AF480304

CUT AND SAVE THE LINE

CUT AND SAVE THE LINE

ALEX NOLOS

"I'm no longer a fucked-up female.
Hallelujah! I'm now a fucked-up male!!"
-Lou Sullivan

I

2015

The train pulled into the station like it was ashamed of being thirty minutes late, but delays on this line were so frequent that it was Lis's expectation of timeliness that was actually shameful. It was so hot and close on that platform that it felt as if the air itself were exhausted and leaning on her for support. She was not eager to get to her destination, but she *was* eager to get into a subway car for the air conditioning. The train that screeched to a stop had candy-corn conversation seating. Lis preferred these to the blue tube cars that lacked window seats. Though there was nothing to look at on her route, she still enjoyed looking out the window at the dark tunnels and her own faint reflection on the glass. She liked to turn her head in different angles to see if any of them worked. It was eleven AM on a weekday.

Her boyfriend would be waiting for her on the terrace between the two campus buildings, but she wouldn't go to him right away. She'd stop to treat herself to something sweet and caffeinated at the campus Starbucks, which would stall her for at least fifteen more minutes. The art majors would have finished putting up their latest projects in the hallway that morning, so she could stop and look for a while and collect another five to seven minutes. It was nice to admire the talent of the other students, as if she'd ever meet them. Though the school was small, it was easy to avoid interacting with people outside of her major.

She and her boyfriend had been paired up for a scene study from *Who's Afraid of Virginia Woolf* by their acting professor; whether or not he knew they were dating was unknown, as they did not advertise this fact. They didn't need to—the school was small enough and straight men in such short supply that all couples were recorded on a well-disseminated verbal census. But the professor was an adjunct, and had not the time nor the energy to memorize his students' names. Her boyfriend thought that this was an advantage. Their relationship would make their scene better, their natural chemistry would feed into their performances and make them seem like a real married couple. Lis tried to delicately explain that, as she understood it, these characters hated each other and the husband was likely a closeted homosexual, but he could not be convinced, and in acting the part of a loving yet tormented husband the rehearsals they had were so painful that Lis tried to make them go by as quickly as possible to avoid having to diagnose the issue. Lately, she'd been trying to inspire dramatic conflict by creating thorny little problems,—like being half an hour late to a twenty minute read-through—hoping that it would give the scene the meanness it required.

This boyfriend, Tyler, seemed to come out of nowhere. Before him, she hadn't dated since grade four. Throughout high school and her first two years of college, she'd had plenty of crushes, but was never able to turn them into anything more. Tyler, like a wish come true, was a composite of all the boys she'd crushed on before: a consummate theater kid, clean and shiny-toothed with the air and exuberance of a pastor's son spliced with a jack russell, and often mistaken for gay to boot, unlike many of her previous crushes who had been actually gay and thus unavailable to her. He was Tyler, in every sense of the name. She wasn't in love with him yet, but she thought she might be if given the time. They could be an artist couple, growing old and bent with memories of fabulous productions to reminisce on, but she also knew that the odds of her finding a lifelong partner at this age were slim. They'd met as freshmen, when the playing field felt very even, as if everyone was in the same league because they had only just started to size each other up for competition. During orientation, Lis's roommate Madison pulled them together by the hand to force a greeting, telling Lis about how Tyler was from the same town in Vermont as her and was "like, her literal brother," and gushing to Tyler about how Lis was her brand-new roommate and the nicest person she'd ever met. For the first two years of school, Lis and Tyler circled each other, teased by Madison and Silvia, Lis's other roommate. They were often left alone together, as if their friends were scientists leaving bacteria in a dish to see what would happen, but they had never kept in touch over breaks until a few months ago, before the start of their junior year. Lis was not particularly dazzled by Tyler, but he was nice, and cute enough, and willing, so she asked him if he would go out with her after they'd finished unpacking their dorms. He agreed, and they'd been together since the beginning of the semester. She hoped that if they were going to break up, it'd be in the summer, so she wouldn't have to see him around for a while, and if they were going to have sex at some point, she hoped it wouldn't happen right before the breakup.

It would still be September for a little while; soon she'd get to decorate her dorm with Silvia and Madison for Halloween. The train's air conditioning was still on, thanks to the brutality of summer and its length. Every place she went was hot and wet, and she feared the days when late fall overlapped with radiator season, when it'd be hot, wet, and smell like being trapped in an unventilated room with a dryer that ran day and night. Winter was far enough off that the idea of it was a ghost story. Silvia, her roommate, was fine with heat. She was in the dance major, and the cold was dangerous for her muscles. Lis, who never danced, could only imagine how the cold tightened up strings in the body so that they'd snap when doing the necessary moves that made dancers what they were: throwing their legs up in the air (snapped hamstring), arms above heads (busted funny bones), twirling around at the hips (shredded obliques).

In her first year, Lis was scared of the subway. She knew that if she was going to be attacked, this would be where. The columns that smelled like piss and the stench of the silt under the tracks gave her clues about what happened here at night; she would only get on after dark if she were with friends, like her mother told her to. Once, Madison pulled her out of the way of a drunk man who'd been about to walk up behind her and put his arms around her while they waited for a train to their afternoon chemistry lab. Madison speed-walked her down the platform for ten feet or so before telling her what had almost happened so that Lis wouldn't freak out. They outpaced the grabber, whisking away at triple his speed. When Lis looked back and Madison pointed him out, he was looking the other way, like he'd forgotten what he'd tried to do. He looked so innocent that Lis wondered for a moment if Madison should be believed. Maybe she'd overreacted, with Madison that was always a possibility.

Once she got settled in her seat, Lis got a feeling like the one she got on long car rides. Being in subtle motion like this felt like a break from life. She was enjoying the time to zone out and breathe for a while, but her stop came too soon. The commute from the dorms to the campus building was only twenty minutes by subway. She got off the train at 68th and walked the long Manhattan blocks to school. As she'd anticipated, the art majors were still in the hallway with tacks, the coffee transaction at the Starbucks popped up on her bank app, and Tyler was waiting, only slightly disgruntled, on the terrace. He looked up from his script to ask what had happened, with only confusion in his voice. It looked like he'd been clutching the photocopied scene in his hands the whole time he'd been waiting; the paper was was warped and stained by his sun-warmed fingerprints. Lis hoped that meant he knew his lines. "Sorry, the train was delayed and I couldn't get service to text you. I brought you this." She handed him an iced tea, since he wouldn't drink caffeine if it was in coffee.

When she announced which college she wanted to take out loans for, her mother said, "God, you're never going to get a boyfriend," which made landing Tyler all the more satisfying. She couldn't figure out why there were hardly any straight men at her school, but she didn't necessarily mind. Madison had been rabid to have them get together. Madison often, without provocation, let Lis know that he'd never said he was gay despite the warm, tolerant environment Madison painstakingly created for him. Madison would then go on about what a liberal and accepting friend she was, opening the closet door at every juncture for Tyler walk through, but he wouldn't, and Lis couldn't help but think Madison was a touch insulted by this. Tyler was a very easy boyfriend, and she didn't have to maintain him with affection, which was currently working against her, foiling her scheme to make their scene presentation better. The way he acted sometimes made her wonder if he even existed when she wasn't around. His behavior sometimes reminded her of how parents will start children off with a goldfish before letting them have a dog.

Knowing Tyler was different than she expected it to be. Her prior crushes were all boys that she'd grown up with, and now that she was away from them she understood how disappointing it would have been to be with any of them. She knew too much about those boys; she knew all their embarrassing stories, the times they'd farted in class or gotten hard during group projects. She knew which ones were bad dates and which ones were scary dates, and she knew which ones were actually very sweet but too embarrassing to be around in public. Tyler was a mystery at first, and everything she'd since learned about him was inoffensive. He was an acting major like her, but he could sing. He'd tried out for musical theater and was so good they offered him the Acting BFA, which he worried would upset Madison since she'd been his favorite co-star in all their high school shows. She was Mme. Thenardier when he was Valjean, she was Titania when he was Puck, she was laughed at when he was applauded, a pattern that persisted into adulthood. Lis used to wonder if Madison was in love with Tyler, but she soon realized that no, not romantically or sexually she wasn't, but in a more possessive way. In the way that she intended to be his children's godmother, not their mother. This explained why, when Lis and Tyler got together, Madison was sharp despite her delight, saying "Oh good! I already like you so that makes this easier." Madison was the only thing that scared Lis about the inevitable end of her relationship.

She took a seat next to him on the bench, the sun shining directly in her eyes. She realized with poor hindsight that they shouldn't have skipped out on booking rehearsal space. The terrace was crowded and it was still hot, she sucked down big sips of iced coffee to keep her cool, but she wouldn't have enough to last her for the time it took to go through their scene. Tyler accepted the iced tea from her and straightened his papers, then noticed Lis's empty hands. "Are you off-book?"

Lis nodded, she'd been off-book for weeks and only today decided to leave her script at home so as not to shame him. "Yep."

They read through the scene. It was a good one, the one where she got to say "what a dump." Lis didn't like doing this with him, pretending to be an old jaded couple. She wanted to come at a scene with no baggage, to do it with a stranger. This would be going so much better if the professor had coupled her with one of the gays in her class, someone who actually could act like a closeted middle-aged man, and she'd be able to do the Elizabeth Taylor part more justice. For one little line, she had to sing. It didn't have to be good since both of these characters were drunk, but she still had to do it and it annoyed her when

Tyler gave her sideways glances that her pitch was off when it wasn't even supposed to be on. Any one of the MT majors she could have been paired with would give her the same glance, but with Tyler, she had to talk to him, text him, take pictures with him, go on dates with him, remembering the glances and forbidding them from bothering her. She knew they should be blocking movement or at least standing up while they read, but instead they sat on the bench, sweating and reading through the scene over and over again, sipping their drinks.

As some clouds rolled in, a breeze picked up and made her more comfortable. Tyler delivered his lines like he was in *Guys and Dolls*. She wondered if the acting major was the right choice for him. Though it came with more prestige and brag-ability, she thought he might be happier in MT. He'd be great in a show someday. He could be the boring guy in *Kinky Boots*, or the boring guy in *How to Succeed in Business Without Really Trying*, or any role in *The Music Man*. He had all the makings of a Tony-winning leading man with disposable income who no one without a Backstage account would ever hear of, including the three-piece midwestern evangelical name: Tyler Hunter Thomas. Little dark spots pecked at the concrete, it had started to rain. Tyler offered to move the reading inside, but Lis was sick of it and knew that she wouldn't be doing this again unless they got a rehearsal room. She declined, pointing out that he had to get to class in only ten minutes. He leaned in to kiss her goodbye. Kissing still made her nervous. Every time they did it, she had the fear that she'd sneeze on him, drool, or clack her head on his too fast and break his nose.

The scene they'd been assigned was something they were

supposed to chew on for the entire semester. The idea was for them to start working on it now, workshop it a bit in class, and then by the time they were ready to do the last run, they'd synthesize almost everything they'd learned. Then, they'd be thrown into preparation for auditions. Most acting majors got their first part at the end of their sophomore year. Lis hadn't made it past the second round of callbacks last spring, nor the first round the year before that. The rejection didn't just sting, it haunted her. Still, when she considered herself, things were generally fine. Lis thought she was a good foreteller; she could spot cracks ready to open, and pull the divide together before things fell through, even if they got snagged in the seam. She was what she'd describe as "very comfortable." In the mirror, she made lists: pretty, talented, and soon-to-be educated. In sum: doing well.

2017

Ty never saw himself going stealth. He didn't mean to, but he'd accidentally adopted a "don't ask, don't tell" policy for himself whereby an interested co-worker was welcome to the knowledge of his transness, but he was not looking for opportunities to bring it up. When he used to work at the cafe, he found himself coming out four or five times a day. It was a different beast, to be corralled behind a coffee counter, in close quarters with everyone he worked with. There it would have been impossible to spend eight hours a day with nothing to do during down time but talk without telling them. But in the five months he'd been at his new job, his schedule was stacked. He had his own cubicle, with a big slow computer and a phone, the model of which reminded him of every doctor's appointment at which he'd spent upwards of 45 minutes talking to the front desk, trying to work out insurance codes and other nonsense he could never defeat. There was once a miserable time in his life where he spoke to Medicaid reps more than anyone else—but he was grateful for it, he had to be.

This new job was much easier, yet he maintained a high baseline of daily stress. Ty wondered if the problem was that he wasn't built to be at ease. Even so, the job felt like a reward for putting up with years of being harangued by ghoulish customers whose questions and comments ranged from the inane to the abusive. To date, no one at this job had called him a worthless cunt and/or faggot, a step up to be sure. In fact, Ty no longer needed to speak to customers at all, instead picking up the phone only to talk to other departments, and at odd intervals through the day swiveling in his chair to exchange remarks with the rest of the team. They were altogether a young bunch; it was made clear to him that most folks in his department were passing through, using this place as a springboard to bigger and better jobs. Ty was content. In the time he'd been plucking spreadsheets for them, he'd grown to truly love the peace and stability of a nine to five. Sometimes, it felt cruel to come home every day at the same time and have weekends off when everyone else he knew had either too much or too little work, and rarely did they get two days off in a row. Even working at the cafe had been a cakewalk compared to what others could get. Nat, who'd taken Ty's old job when he left, only complained in short bursts, knowing better than to rant and rave when he got paid above minimum wage, and Nat rarely knew better than to act above his own impulses. Nat knew quite little, period.

Nat moved out of his school's dorms and into Ty and Max's apartment when his graduation timed nicely with the departure of Ty's former roommate, who was getting married to a woman neither Ty nor Max had ever seen. Somehow, it was decided that Nat moving in was the most logical move, though Ty was the last to agree, for reasons he would rather have stayed in denial about. The association between Ty and Nat was a source of mixed anguish, embarrassment, and humor at Ty's expense. It had only been a few months that Nat had been living with them, and so far it was fine. They were all friends (officially) and all hung out in the same places, and Nat participated in the life of the apartment that their old roommate opted out of. Before Nat, Ty and Max usually forgot they had a third bedroom, but Nat made such an effort to be out and about and a part of everything that there was practically an open invitation for either one to sleep on his floor if they felt like it. Max was warm towards Nat, and though Ty didn't feel forced to agree to let Nat move in, he rejected the odd big brother role that he felt was imposed on him, a dynamic he knew Nat certainly didn't appreciate.

Nat was a lucky bastard. He'd been able to start testosterone the year prior, and his puberty came on fast. It was like he went home to Jersey in the summer of 2016 and incubated into a full grown man, like a trans fag Venus on the half-shell. By fall, he was passing cleanly, even on the phone. Ty still got ma'am-ed three out of every five calls he made. Ty would have been jealous if Nat's newness didn't make him feel lucky to have spent his first three years out of the closet without friends. Nat hadn't gotten himself into real trouble yet, but only because his dumb-est utterances had been said in the presence of those who would cut him some slack, but Ty feared that at some point Nat would shove his foot in his mouth while at one of Max's shows in front of someone who would neither humor him nor chalk up his fool-ishness to that of the nouveau queer. Though Ty was not exactly happy to have Nat around so much, he did feel that the night-life scene was a good environment to grow up in. Nat needed to be challenged, to have the ideas he absorbed from years of on-line lurking pulled into the light and questioned. Ty was curious about the kind of person he was due to become.

He was expecting a call from his pharmacy, so he anxiously glanced at his phone every few minutes, hoping that he wouldn't be in the middle of anything when the phone rang, because if he missed it he would have to sit through the hold music for thirty minutes. He'd heard that hold music so many times that if he sat down and summoned his third-grade music class training he could put in on a staff and play it on the flutophone. Real-istically, he knew that he wouldn't hear from them, and instead the best thing to do would be to show up at the pharmacy and throw his pleading face at the problem. Having a prescription for a controlled substance meant that he could not get refills; every time he ran out of testosterone he had to ask his doctor to write a brand-new prescription, inviting chaos. His clinic was a Safe Space, a queer community health center that had been on the frontlines of the health crises facing local queers since the eighties. It had history that gave it prestige, but neither of those things brought in the kind of funding they needed, and with the overcrowding, they needed a lot. Patient openings were coveted, and the location in lower Manhattan only accepted new patients a few times a year. Nat had only gotten off the waiting list recently, prior to that he made the hours long commute to their other location in the Bronx, and at the very beginning of his T regimen he had to go there every week to be injected by a nurse before he was allowed to do it at home. When Ty started, the Bronx location didn't exist, but he spent an amount of time equivalent to the Bronx commute just sitting in the pharmacy waiting room while a belabored pharmacist tried to work with his insurance. Those hours were in vain—insurance did not cover his prescription, and every five months he shelled out $70 to avoid the consequences of suddenly withdrawing from the hormone he'd been self-stimulating for the past four years. It shouldn't be so hard to get these things in order; he wondered if maybe the pharmacy had such an incredible rate of staff turnover that there was never a day where the person on site had ever met a transsexual before.

Tweet notifications lit up Ty's phone. Nothing he wanted to see, just retweets to Nat's page about something or other being valid. Ty did not necessarily believe in the adage that one got more conservative as one got older, but Nat made him feel spiteful. Nat had just gotten his top surgery date, a milestone that increased the frothiness of his tweeting and general presence. Ty was looking forward to Nat's surgery, hoping that it would make him shut up. He was also looking forward to it because he hoped that Nat would decide to spend his recovery at home in New Jersey. He did not want to feel obligated to care for Nat, helping him strip his drains and telling him what his incisions should look like at each stage of healing. Ty knew the surgeon Nat was going to because the same one had done his own surgery years ago. What was worse than Nat going to the same surgeon was that he didn't even know who Ty's was before the consultation, he'd just serendipitously picked her out from the massive roster of low-profile top surgeons in New York. Nat made little jokes about being "chest buds" with Ty.

By the time Ty left work, he still hadn't heard back from his pharmacy, and he let himself forget to nudge them. For once, he'd like it if the clinic chased *him* down.

2

2015

Lis lived with Silvia and Madison on the fourth floor of the dorms. The building was co-ed, but the rooms were segregated by sex. Though the journey home was usually quick once off the train, the elevators were out of service, so the eight-story building was a walk-up for the time being. Madison and Silvia, did fine with the climb, but Lis was out of breath and dizzy by the time she got to the third level. Madison bought her a giant, probably expensive, bottle of iron supplements and told her the right dosing schedule for her BMI.

The dorms were one-bedroom apartments made to accomodate three to four people. Each unit had a kitchenette and a small living room; generous for dorms, unacceptable for off-campus living. To accomodate three people in one bedroom, Madison and Lis shared an L-shaped bunk bed, and Silvia took a loft. Each student was promised a desk, which might have been nice, but the school chose to squeeze them into the bedrooms so that every piece of furniture touched. Every night, Lis slept hedged in by her desk on one side, Silvia's on the other, and Madison sleeping above her. She took the only low bed so she wouldn't need to deal with a ladder, but it meant that she couldn't see the window at night, which bothered her more than she thought it would have. The upside was that she didn't make much noise if she wanted to get up at night, which she did, frequently. Lis went to bed early, but didn't stay in it.

Once in the door, Trevor greeted her from the couch. Trevor was yet another MT major, (musical theater was the school's most popular major, since it'd been a checkpoint for a good number of Tony winners who'd stopped in, dropped out, and gone on to be cast in much-raved about productions) and since he lived on the top floor, he would stop in their room to catch his breath and linger on the way home. He didn't have a key or anything, but they were thinking of breaking school rules to make him one since they'd each had the experience of coming home to find Trevor slumped in front of their door imitating a dried-out pilgrim awaiting rescue. Madison was sitting on the very edge of the couch, her body language that of someone who'd not been expecting a guest. She behaved this way every time Trevor came by, though she craved his friendship deeply and was always trying to impress him. On seeing Lis, she asked, "How'd rehearsal go? Tyler said you were coming home to work on a chem thing." Lis was used to this, the surveillance that came from living with your boyfriend's closest friend. The chem thing was an online mini-quiz based on a chapter of the textbook that had an answer sheet easily found via Google; every STEM class was designed to be passable for theater majors. It was an assignment that would take Lis five minutes to do, but Madison didn't need to know that. Madison was nosy, but not very attentive.

Lis let her bag go, took her cardigan off, and plopped down next to Trevor on the peninsula of the school-issued sectional, then sighed and said in a strained voice, "Yeah, Sampoli's kicking my ass." She didn't make it into the acting major without reason.

Trevor said, "I know that *everyone* has to do gen-ed science but really who do they think they're kidding? Like we're going to have a dark crisis of the soul one night and switch to bio with the other four in that major," to which Madison replied, "I think they don't want us to be stupid. What if you have to play a scientist or something someday?" Trevor considered this. "Right, that makes sense."

Silvia got home. She, like all the other dance majors, was always sweating. They tended to sweat in an even sheen, not fat greasy bulbs down the face like most people did. The dancers didn't wear buns all the time like Lis thought they were supposed to; Silvia took hers down as soon as she got out of class to preserve her hairline, and it worked. Her hairline sat about two inches further down than most of the other dancers, so she didn't look like a lightbulb. She washed her hair every night because of all the sweat, but it didn't dry out, because of all the sweat. Her bun held back what looked like six pounds of tight curls. She was undoubtedly the prettiest person Lis knew, and addictive to be around. Silvia said hello and came over to give Trevor a cheek kiss. Silvia and Trevor were very close. It was intense when they were out together, like they were stars of their own variety show —Sonny and Cher but with two Chers. They went out often. Afterward, they'd come home to the girls' dorm and fall asleep on the couch, still talking, passing out mid-sentence. In the mornings they stank horribly, but looked great. Trevor stained the couch cushion one night with mascara, so they'd had to flip it over, leaving one cushion a shade paler than the others.

Lis wished she was invited out with Silvia and Trevor more often, as she didn't like being left alone with Madison. It was easy to get tired of her. Lis felt bad for her in a lot of ways, including for the pity she brought out in Lis. Madison just seemed so desperate for everything—grades, attention, compliments, beauty, friends, talent—that Lis couldn't help but think mean things and immediately feel guilty for thinking them. Trevor was not shy about teasing her, but they still got along moderately well, and there were plenty of nights (especially when Trevor and Silvia were gone) that Lis stayed up with her and enjoyed the conversation, but then the next day Madison would huff around the dorm, walking into a room and making faces to indicate someone should ask her what was going on, or launch into uninvited descriptions of the various issues she was having with professors, the arguments she'd won in class, and other contrived victories and losses from the day. From the way she behaved, it was clear she spent much of her time trying to create a story of herself that would be as interesting to everyone else as it was to her, but very little time making that story true. When Lis really thought about it, *really* thought about it, she saw Madison as someone trapped inside of herself. It was like there was a layer of keratin around a calm, enjoyable version of her that could to be filed down to free her, but how would you do that? Lis could only imagine terrible things, insults or fights to show Madison what people didn't like about her, but that would be cruel. She didn't want to get to the good parts of Madison by ripping off everything else. So, Lis tried to accept Madison for who she was, and slipped in a tease or a joke at her unwitting expense here and there, waiting for the moment that Madison might snap and understand.

After some chatting, Lis drifted to her desk. She pulled up a tab on her laptop for the chemistry quiz, and between answering each question, she checked a different website. After number one, she refreshed Tumblr, after two she checked Facebook, etc. The next stop was YouTube. A British beauty vlogger had just uploaded a new video, a long one, clocking in at eleven minutes. When Lis pulled it up, the recommended bar on the side showed her a thumbnail for "Debunking Testosterone Myths." It wasn't like Silvia or Madison would know what that meant, but to be safe Lis hit fullscreen to hide it. These videos got put in front of her all the time, due to certain viewing habits. Since she'd left home, she'd cut back, but she couldn't reset the algorithm unless she cleared her watch history, and she didn't want to. The thumbnail of the video was a tiny window into the bedroom/ filming space of a blue-haired man she knew well. She'd watched dozens of his videos. It was how she already knew which testos-terone myths he was going to debunk in the video. Anger issues, hair loss, "growth," etc. She used to watch videos of his and a few other guys all the time at home, when she had her own bedroom. Now she was busier, and had less privacy.

As if to confirm her paranoia, Madison bust in and said in a rush: "Hey do you have plans on Saturday Trevor asked us to go to a drag show with him and Silvia in Brooklyn." It was not a question, but a herald, like she was playing the town crier. Lis couldn't say no even if she lost her mind and wanted to. An in-vitation. A drag show. Brooklyn. This was what she moved here for. "Yes, absolutely."

2017

It took about forty-five minutes to get home, on a good day. Today was not a good day, so Ty walked off the train car ninety minutes after leaving work and hustled his way between people caught in the same delay with even more distance to travel. A man was screaming to no one in particular; he was only partaking in the necessary steam-letting required to let the world know there was a problem with no sincere expectation that it would be fixed. Ty saw a water bottle someone had left on the stairs and kicked it off to the side; he always worried that someone would step on one and roll their ankle or that an old woman would lose her footing on it and break a hip. If he saw it, it naturally became his responsibility to fix it, and his fault if he ignored it and someone got hurt.

At least it only took fifteen minutes to get home once he got off the train. As he came up the stairs, he heard music so loud and so perfume-pop he couldn't be sure if he was opening his front door or the door to an H&M. Ty rattled his keys out of his pockets and found both Max and Nat, sitting but not talking. Before he could ask if they were giving him an intervention, they talked over each other to explain that one of their shared favorite pop stars had just dropped a new single and that this was their third listen. Ty nodded and dropped his things off, heading to his room to change out of his work clothes. He picked his jewelry off the dish on his nightstand and put it back in his face; he was too self-conscious to wear it to work, but he didn't want the holes to close since he did think he looked better with it on. When he changed shirts, his tattoos returned to his body. He looked like himself again, though he sometimes felt like a parody of himself. To see how he looked now in comparison to how he looked at work was jarring, so he usually avoided mirrors during the day, but he couldn't help facing the window when he was stuck on the train. He'd stared at himself in the car's window, wishing he could see if his arm veins were apparent as he held the ceiling rail. It was frustrating, how office clothes never failed to make him small and ridiculous.

After re-dressing, he considered kicking around the litter on his floor, detritus from last week's Pride that he wasn't in the mood to clean up yet. Pins, ribbons, glitter that came off of Nat and Max and Silvia and Lita's bodies—truly, any body but his—formed a layer of silt. Maybe the reason for the hold up at his pharmacy was because Pride awakened some things in some people and caused an influx of new patients. The song in the other room ended and started again. Ty recognized the voice as one that sang through speakers all last week, a sweet frying lilt that could alternately whisper and wail. Max and Nat weren't the only ones obsessed. They'd asked drivers for AUX cords to play her album when all five of them crammed in for late night drives between shows, marches, and home. Max sang along, Nat didn't. He'd been insecure about his singing voice since childhood. Ty remembered when he told him that, he wasn't sure who else knew.

Ty used to confine himself to his room. Besides sleeping, he would also eat, entertain, and brood from his bed. It was why he had the habit of keeping his windows open, to stop it from smelling like a cave. For all the clutter in those four walls, he was obsessive about keeping the windows clean. He kept his own bottle of Windex under his desk with a roll of paper towels and performed the task every other day. It was more necessary when he used to smoke, now it was a compulsion. He approached the window, pulled it and the bug screen apart from the sill, and stuck his legs out onto the fire escape. The metal frame bit into the back of his thighs. Sometimes he still wished he smoked, just to give him something to do. It had been a rainy summer; he could feel little bits of moisture diffuse into his jeans. Then, a knock at the door. Nat. "Are you good if I shower?" Nat always opened the door too wide, but stood at the threshold like a polite vampire, barely concealing how vital it was for him to be invited in. His twinky frame let too much light into the room even when standing right in the frame. "Go ahead," he said, dismissing Nat. Nat pulled the door shut, and with an extra tug due to the humidity, the latch clicked. Solitude restored.

Max could be heard in the kitchen, still looping the song she'd been listening to with Nat, but now focusing on preparations for her dinner. She ate more vegetables than anyone Ty knew; he never saw a starch enter her body. It would worry him, if she weren't completely ripped to shreds. Anyone that strong had to be building muscle with something. Ty chalked his own lack of definition up to not eating enough, rather than his refusal to train. The first time he saw Nat after he'd gone on hormones, he already had thicker arms, just from the daily efforts of, Ty supposed, lifting iced coffees off of bar counters and playfully pushing people on the arm. Now, Ty probably couldn't pin Nat down that easily, which he'd realized fairly recently and tried not to think too much about.

Ty continued to sit at his window, observing the stillness of the alley and the broken bottles thrown down by their second-floor neighbor. From the top of the building, Ty watched as nothing underneath him changed except for one spot, a rancid rotting amorphous shape in the concrete produced by a gutter near the back. From where he was, no smell could be detected, but he knew that the ground floor tenants were in a long-running war with the landlord to have the gutters either professionally cleaned or removed entirely since everything that passed through it became corrosive and smelled like sulfur and ammonia. His neighbor thought it was birds pissing directly into the drain on the roof. Ty didn't know much about zoology, but thought was unlikely. The spot on the concrete had been growing for months, and just recently, after an extremely hot day in the first week of June, part of the ground split. Surrounding the seam was a broad, rust and oil colored sprawling patch. It was always wet.

The air smelled metallic, like a thunderstorm. Ty pulled his legs in, waited for the sound of the bathroom faucet, then went to chat with Max while she butchered bok choy and layered spices.

3

The thought of getting on the train so late frightened Lis, but she thought maybe they could get a car ride back if they split it. The bar was called Chrome, which made Lis think of sleekness and Manhattan, but it was in Williamsburg. Perfect, she'd always wanted to see it, but the only parts of Brooklyn she'd ever been to was DUMBO. It was colder than the preceding week's heat had suggested it would be, and Lis shivered in her skirt. She was wearing skirts more often lately. The more she did, the less difficult it was. It wasn't the skirt that was hard, it was the tights and the underwear and the bike shorts; all the layers she needed to keep herself safe. A skirt at home was the most comfortable thing, she could move however she wanted to. On the subway she had to sit just so, with her knees tight together, but not crossed. She was twelve when she learned that crossing your legs was promiscuous; prior to that she thought it was the most direct way to guard herself, but she never noticed that with one thigh up, skirts fell back to show your ass. Having to sit correctly in so many layers of fabric made her both dry and sweaty, and getting undressed once home was unsatisfying. The tights and shorts could hardly be called dirty, having been in contact only with each other or other fabric, but they took on the shape of dirty clothes, creased and baggy.

Off the train, down the elevated platform. She'd never been on an elevated platform before, except for the bridges, if those counted. They walked down to the sidewalk, and it felt like the inverse of getting off the train near the dorms. For the people who lived along this line, home was on the lower level. Once on the street, it was a short, chilly, giggling walk to the bar. Lis, the only one wearing a skirt, made it inside with gooseflesh legs that warmed up in the plastic breezeway where they waited to be waved in. Part of the appeal here was that they didn't card—a good place for her to be twenty and a good place for the owners to get money from college students. The interior was not what Lis had been expecting, but she tried to roll with it. It was smaller, it was dirtier, it did not live up to its name. But this was Brooklyn, a cooler, nastier place where things were rougher and realer than she was used to, she said to herself. She hoped she wouldn't need to use the bathroom, since it clearly had no lock and one's privacy would rely on the honor system. Despite the hope of keeping her bladder dry, she accepted a vodka soda from Trevor, who was already 21.

Who were the queens here? The cast was supposed to be small, but the room was full of people in outfits that could be costumes. This was the Brooklyn drag she'd heard so much about. She hadn't expected to see so many women, based on the handful of visits she'd made to gay bars in Manhattan, but there were plenty of girls around. It seemed that everyone was here;

if you were looking for someone, you'd be able to find them or their composite. Unless you were looking for a Lis, or a Madison. They each noticed their mismatched energy at the same time, and their excitement turned to self-consciousness. Madison took more frantic sips of her drink.

Lis watched Trevor and Silvia break away and mingle with the crowd. It seemed like they knew everyone, and Trevor kissed several people on the mouth as a greeting, which Lis had never seen before. While she watched them and checked her phone out of nervous habit, someone came over to her. Once she noticed him approach, she took note of his height, and the fact that he did not look like what she expected gay men to look like. In fact, in his demeanor she saw something that told her he might be approaching with interest. So far, Madison had made seven jokes about the appeal of gay bars as places where she wouldn't be hit on, but once Lis got a good look at the man walking up to her, she thought she noticed something, and tried not to be too pleased with herself out of the fear of being wrong. As he got closer, she felt her heart fall through her body like a pinball. A bewildering exhilaration flew through her head as she got the sensation that something many years in the making was headed her way. She also noticed that his lips were chapped, and that the dead skin was dyed purple by whatever he'd been drinking. Or maybe it was from candy? No, candy was too childish. Well, it wasn't the candy eating that would be childish, but the messy eating that stains lips. Lips stained by a drink though, that was not childish, that was romantic. It was sexy. He had a few tattoos, some nicer than others, and from what she could tell, all pretty dissimilar.

It bothered her to see different styles collaged onto one body, but in the light of the bar they looked good together.

He smiled, and asked who she'd come with. *Ah,* she thought, *I stick out, he's wondering how I got here.* She pointed to Trevor, currently dancing up against a tall ghostly blond. The man looked and said, "Trevor? Oh. Yeah, I don't know him that well. My roommate is the host."

"Oh, that's so cool. Are they here already?" She was proud of herself for remembering to say *they.*

"Yeah, Max, the host? She's right there." Lis felt ignorant; this information was probably all over an Instagram post she could have looked at before coming. She'd given away that she didn't know what she was here for. He pointed, but she couldn't tell who was supposed to catch her attention. The tall blue-painted woman in sunglasses and gauze? Or the Sharon Stone lookalike in leather? "She's great. Have you not seen this show before?"

"Uh no, I don't actually get to Brooklyn much." She wondered if he could hear the *at all* in her voice. He said that he was here all the time, and asked if this was her first drag show. It was, but she was embarrassed that she was so obviously *new.* Again, she stammered, and haltingly explained that she'd seen many drag shows online. She could have lied, but he might ask which show she'd been to. She was losing the conversation quickly. She wanted to keep his attention but she had nothing interesting to say. Just out of view, she saw Madison squinting and glaring at her, wondering what was going on. Lis was terrified that she might come over and embarrass her. A desperate feeling took hold; how could she re-arrange herself in the next thirty seconds to put distance between herself and Madison? As her brain shifted to worry about the people she was with, the conversation fizzled out, and he told her to enjoy the show before going back over to his friends, a group of similarly-tattooed people who were all very attractive, but who didn't appeal to her as much. Lis saw one of them say, "struck out again?" and then she looked away so he could answer honestly.

Madison came and wrangled her. "Making friends?" She asked. Lis gave a vague response and then the host, Max, who turned out to be the blue woman, took the stage. Trevor and Silvia came to retrieve their friends and direct them to a booth. Lis couldn't remember the guy's name, or if he even gave it, and because of this, she couldn't sit through the show peacefully, though she could tell that she would have enjoyed it otherwise. Each act gave the audience plenty to look at: confetti, good taste in music, dancing, blood. She'd never seen anything like this before, but it felt like she had, for all of it seemed so natural. The guy she'd talked to and his friends stood for the show, whereas Trevor and Silvia had them sit at back, and it embarrassed her; she worried that it looked like they were trying to be better than everyone else there. She kept thinking of Trevor as their guide, the person who made it okay for them to be here, even though he'd immediately broken off from them once they got in the door. By simply being the gay to extend the invitation, Trevor had created the circumstances for her to see this, to feel cool, to meet that guy. She should be grateful. Lis sat quietly, laughing when Max—a good host, funny and brief—made jokes, staring in awe at the right moments, but she felt guilty for spending the show in wait and not in rapture. After thirty minutes, Max announced intermission, to Lis's gratitude.

Trevor looked at the white-hot glow from various messaging apps on his phone and, while reading his notifications, said, "Ok I'm getting drinks, but you two should find places to use the bathroom." Silvia asked what was wrong with the bar's bathroom. "You're fine, these two are anxious pissers." Madison nodded vigorously, looking relieved that Trevor had given her a momentary out, but Lis didn't want to leave, to go out and find a private bathroom that locked and smelled clean. Madison tugged on her arm and made her put on her jacket. It was cold outside, another reason to stay in and hold it or suck it up and brave the bar bathroom or maybe just wait till they got home to the dorms, but when Madison started to head out, Lis caved. Besides, Trevor was right about their shy bladders and after the drink she'd had, sitting through another act of the show would be impossible.

Madison pointed to a little pink spot on the corner, some sort of late night bakery. It would do. Madison began to eagerly discuss the show. "It's fucking freaky, right?"

"It's so good."

"Oh yeah yeah, not freaky like weird. Like, it's new."

"Mm-hmm."

"You okay?"

"Yeah, it's just fucking *cold.*"

"You shouldn't have worn a skirt!" Madison laughed. "What, you thought you were going to pick someone up tonight? Tyler not doing it for you?"

Madison was joking, but only a little. She'd clearly seen the conversation Lis had been having earlier. Instead of thinking to dispel Madison's suspicion, Lis was relieved that the conversation looked like flirting from another's eyes. Maybe she *could* pick someone up tonight and surprise them, her friends, piss Madison off and watch her turn red. Maybe that guy in the bar could still be impressed after the failure of their first conversation. Maybe she could spin around in her skirt a little, maybe he'd like it. Madison would tell Tyler, but that would be okay. She wasn't scared of him, neither his anger nor the loss of him. In fact, it might be the inspiration he needed to pull off their scene. Lis tended to get high off spite, and just then she wanted to turn back and make a reckless decision, but she still felt responsible for escorting Madison to the cafe, to stand outside the door to make sure no one bothered her. A wind blew the skirt around her thighs, exposing the shorts and the thick crotch lining of the tights. Madison squealed at the cold, and the question seemed to be forgotten.

After Madison's turn in the bathroom, Lis told her not to wait outside, as she wouldn't be able to go if she knew Madison was there, tapping her foot. But Madison insisted, as if protecting Lis from herself, as if Lis was going to drown in the toilet unless Madison were there to listen for splashing. Somehow, despite years of well-entrenched bladder anxiety, Lis was irritated enough to piss with fury. When she got out of the bathroom, Madison looked unnerved and asked if Lis was okay.

"Yeah, why?"

"You took forever. Can we look around before we head back?"

The staff were putting up chairs already. Max had said intermission would be ten minutes, they'd already been gone for seven.

"We should go, it's starting again soon."

"Ugh, it's so cold."

Madison dragged her feet the entire way back, adding five more minutes to the walk, guaranteeing that Lis had no chance of talking to anyone at intermission. Max was already back on the mic when they got in. Madison pushed through the small crowd at the very back of the room to sit with Trevor and Silvia where they'd been earlier, but Lis, terribly embarrassed, stood at the back with her coat on. The second act passed like the first, except from where Lis was standing now she could see her guy again. For a moment, he looked at her, closed-lipped smiled at her, and turned back to his friends like it was nothing. Was that flirting, or would flirting look like something different here? Lis couldn't remember how Tyler flirted with her when they met. The people here all seemed to know things she didn't, and she felt inadequate, not like she would never belong here, but like she never should. She was supposed to feel like an alien because that's what she was. It'd be foolish at best and tyrannical at worst to act like she was owed a welcome.

After the show, she regrouped with Madison and Silvia and Trevor. Trevor and Silvia were prepared to stay out for the rest of the night. Lis kept trying to peek around them to look for the guy she'd seen, then regretted being so desperate. Madison tossed out the idea of going to a diner,—she always wanted to go to diners at night,—but it wasn't popular. Trevor and Silvia decided to stay, maybe go to another bar, another show, and Madison turned to Lis. "Well, I guess we'd better head home, huh?" Lis didn't know where Madison got the idea that they weren't allowed to be separated, that if you split their group in two the natural pattern was Trevor and Silvia, Madison and Lis.

Lis resented being grouped with her, but considered how much of an interloper she'd felt like all night. She didn't put up a fight. The dorms, home, that was where she belonged, she was no fun.

Madison was scared of getting on the train without Silvia and Trevor. She argued for taking a car, which would have been over forty dollars, and eventually offered to pay for it. Lis stared out of her window along the ride. The view was beautiful, thanks to shameless rich people with no curtains. Lis peered into the windows of brownstones, then after the bridge, high rises. Though the interiors were all the same,—off-white walls, green plants, and mid-century furniture—Lis couldn't help but be impressed. She wanted to be like that someday, looking out onto cars from a big window day and night, never afraid of what those on the outside could see looking in.

2017

Ty carried a crinkling plaid-print plastic bag full of hair onto the subway. Max had already been at the bar for a while getting set up, but at the last minute she decided that she needed to revisit her wig options because the new one updo she'd intended to debut that night was lifting in the back. Ty often found himself getting to Max's shows early when he had not planned to. Over the course of their friendship, Ty had become Max's unpaid and unofficial assistant, on hand to help her when minor drag emergencies cropped up but not doing such significant labor that he felt he ought to be compensated for his efforts. Besides, Max's emergencies were always minor due to her insistence on denial. Missing the pinky nails of a custom set? Minor. Hecklers? Minor. Fire in the bar? Minor. The piss incident? Minor.

The bag stuck to his arms while he waited on the platform. These trains were usually good, but something about the heat made them slow down. At this hour, it was much more congested, what with people scrambling to make the most of their evenings before the weather turned. Maybe it was the weight of the passengers bearing down on the wheels that made them delay. Ty theorized that the train populace was actually heavier in the summer, since without the bulk of coats and boots more people could be squeezed in, and in his experience, an onboarding passenger did not need much confidence to be willing to test the limits of a car's capacity before stepping on, as if human bodies observed the properties of gas and could simply condense to fit within the confines of their container. The amount of bare strangers' skin that had been pressed up against him in his life might have freaked him out if he hadn't grown up here, but there were many things he accepted without question. To him, things others considered obstacles were trials. Here, for instance, he was not overcrowded, he was conditioned to be a person who could not be disturbed.

When the train showed up he pulled the bag to his front and pressed it to his chest as gently as he could, trying not to take up too much space nor rumple Max's hair. He hated being the person on the train with cargo, so when it happened he tried to be as decent about it as possible. No one's head turned, neither to cast a dirty look for the big bag nor nod in appreciation of his self-containment. It was a signal he broadcast that no one picked up. He was fatigued. The pharmacy still hadn't returned his calls, and it had now been almost three weeks since his last shot. It was getting ridiculous, and at some point he'd have to call them, but he was reluctant. Medical calls never went how he expected them to. Sure, this delay could just be because something fell off the pharmacist's radar, but it could also be because his insurance was up to something again, or because there was a typo on his scrip, or something ridiculous he wouldn't be able to anticipate. These things had not just happened to him before, they were a pattern. Thankfully his vial only needed to be refilled every few months, but three out of every four refill requests came with some kind of drama. He was simply sick of it. And sick literally; he considered this a withdrawal. Really, it was a steep cliff-dive of hormones that threw his whole body out of whack. That morning, he could barely brush his teeth due to ferocious gagging caused by the softest touch of bristles on the back of his throat. He felt so much more vulnerable to the world.

Nights like this were what he needed. Not simply being in the audience, but being useful. Being Max's de facto assistant made him feel like he was earning his keep rather than leeching the energy in the room. To contribute in the ways he was asked to, schlepping wigs around or mending garments or simply being the one to run around the corner and grab a packet of makeup wipes, a phone charger, or Takis was what made him feel like he had any right to be there. The artistry that took place under the roof of the bar sustained him, but he could not create that artistry with his own person. Max's shows were like a canvas tent under a rainstorm, glowing with shelter. People so near to one another they were practically cuddling. In such an environment, Ty felt bonded to even the most unpleasant figures in the room.

At his most jaded, queerness was the mode of life he clung to to feel like he had any free will. When it was more difficult than cathartic, more costly than gratifying, it was still *the* piece of himself that acted as the fulcrum off which he could propel into all other parts of his life. Without being queer, there would be no friends, no apartment, no shows, no work, no clothes, no hair, no sex, no skin, no love. There was no fantasy of a life for him in the straight world. In childhood, before he knew what he was, his imaginings of the future stopped short and tipped over into an abyss he couldn't look into. When he transitioned, he was able to look down into that abyss, and while it was no less mysterious, it was infinitely more possible.

Yet, in recent years, he saw less and less of the friends he originally started going out with. Many had moved, others had schedules that didn't mesh well with his office job, some were lost to bad habits or worse people. His circle was closing in. He tried not to resent this, some of it it was his own fault.

It was a good night, so getting through the door of the bar got more difficult the closer it got to shows, but Ty was early and had no issue slipping in and saying his usual hello to the good bartender (the other one was too eccentric for anyone's taste). He found Max helping a baby queen press on her dominant hand's nails. From the air, Ty sensed that everyone was in a relatively relaxed mood. Lita was helping a queen re-attach an eyelash to a slippery lid. The queen was complaining about how often this happened to her, and Lita told her to start using wig glue. If that failed, she could always ask around and see if there was a filler technician willing to inject Botox into the corners of her eyes. Lita had done drag once, long ago, in a different city. She moved here not to transition, but rather to put a hard boundary between herself as a woman on stage and a woman in real life, as being a trans queen in her hometown made her a too-rare bird, and people could not control themselves, forming an audience even when she was off-duty. Ty didn't know much about Lita, but they got along beautifully. It felt gorgeous to be around her. She did her makeup like it was winter even when it was ninety degrees out, and she was playfully mean enough for her kindness to feel like an honor. Lita had figured out how to strike the delicate balance between jaded and bitter, and her sense of humor made good impressions. When her synapses fired, everyone felt it. If she weren't dating Silvia, Ty thought maybe they could be something, but he was flattering himself.

Being sensitive to heat, Ty preferred winters, but he knew summers were better for his friends. Shows were more crowded, and the more people drank, the more they tipped. Max's usual bar had decent owners, in that while they did take too big of a cut given the condition of the space, they made themselves scarce. There were other places where owners and managers lurked around. There was an old story about one bar owner who had a habit of shoving cameras under people's legs while they went up stairs.

Silvia showed up next, with Nat in tow. Ty remembered when Silvia used to bring her pet fag Trevor instead, but she said Trevor had moved to L.A. a few years ago for boring homosexual reasons. Silvia was the only one of her cohort to have done anything of substance with her degree. She worked with a dance company, performed regularly, and taught classes to children of rich parents in Park Slope for reasonable rates.

Common knowledge was that dancers didn't have much time to make a career before the sport became a danger to their bodies, so it was a relief to Silvia and all who loved her that she'd gotten stable work so quickly. Out on the west coast, Trevor was living a life that seemed to necessitate the marriage of Instagram photos and ad copy for income, and Nat, between cafe shifts, went on auditions every few weeks, but had landed nothing. His current fear was that with "his luck," he'd snag a gig before surgery and have to turn it down. Ty wondered where he got off complaining about *his* luck. Nat's eagerness to get on a stage was bizarre; Ty knew that he was an acting major when they met, but he never seemed that interested in it. Then again, there were many things Nat was not entirely honest about at first.

They lived together, it was unreasonable to try to avoid each other, but Ty tried his best to keep a composed and aloof attitude about him when they were at shows together. Not unlike the image he'd tried to project when Nat was still a stranger to him. When Max was unavailable, Silvia and Lita helped provide a buffer, people that let him feel like Nat was their friend and not his. Unfortunately for Ty, Lita enjoyed watching him and Nat like it was her own personal t-boy ant farm, and she often encouraged bringing Nat along to the few events he wasn't already invited to. She thought that it built character to face your fears, which was the only thing Ty didn't like about her. Lita also genuinely enjoyed Nat, which Ty couldn't understand, but he supposed that ever since Trevor moved, Nat filled the space he left behind.

When Nat and Lita were in one place, whichever of them noticed the other first would scream. That night, it was Lita who peeped over the top of the queen she was assisting to shout, "Baby!" If her finger hadn't been in someone's eye she would have jumped up to run in for a hug. Instead, Nat trotted over, leaving Silvia to mingle on her own. On nights out, Nat often accessorized with his binder. He'd bought a bunch of them in obnoxious fabrics and wore them under mesh overshirts or half-done button-ups. Tonight he had on shiny mermaid-scales under a cropped fishnet hoodie, a garment that struck Ty as two ways to defeat the purpose of a shirt. Even during the day, Nat wore shirts that *just* skimmed the waist of his jeans, so that the slightest movement of his arms exposed slices of his stomach, which was covered in barely perceptible dark blonde hair. Still, Ty felt embarrassingly underdressed in comparison. These nights hadn't been dress-up occasion to him for a long time, but Nat's flamboyance made him regret not making more of an effort.

Max's shows never got old, but maybe just a bit predictable. Surprises were different every time, but it was still a given that there would be surprises. Max was always funny, but Ty had heard most of her jokes before, or at least knew her well enough to predict the punchlines. The crowd was only about fifteen percent different than it had been since Ty had started coming here. Shortly after Nat and Silvia arrived, he gathered with them at the back of the room, letting newcomers and one-time guests have the better views. Nights like these, in places like this, were fun in the most simple way fun can exist, but they were also re- minders. There was no fear in here, and that was a privilege hard- earned, but not by them. Ty thought a lot about the people who came before them, ashamed that his strength had never been put to the test the way theirs had, and even more ashamed for the ingratitude of wishing for that kind of suffering. He forgot he had problems sometimes, because it was easy to think he didn't deserve them. It was easy to become convinced that his good job and safety on the subway meant that he could escape. It was a bizarre trick his mind played on itself: the effort of checking his privilege became the delusion that he could actually become cis. Remembering that that was untrue was a kind of disappointment. There was a mode of cognition he was permanently locked out of, the "cis brain worms" Nat and Lita talked about, a way of thinking that men like him drove alongside but that he was not sure they could cross over into. There were such an unfortunate number of trans men, white trans men, who ended up crashing into the guardrail in an effort to assuage their insecurities. Men who hated women because of the time they'd spent being treated like one. It was a kind of misogyny that upset Ty more than it did coming from cis men, but as he got older, he stopped being surprised by it and instead spent quite a lot of time checking himself for symptoms.

He thought about how much Nat loved Lou Sullivan. Ty loved him too, who wouldn't? His sense of humor, his perverted sensibility, and his oracle-like ability to put down thoughts men like him still had. But Ty was as suspicious of Nat's hero-worship as he was his own. Lou had suffered. Ty wondered if he and Nat and everyone else looked up to Lou for all the right reasons and a little bit of the wrong ones. Lou was historical proof that men like them could be in pain, and he thought that maybe they too often held him up as evidence.

4

All her life, Lis had lived with her family in New Jersey, just an hour away from the city. Her parents sometimes took Lis and her brother on day trips there. Lis always wished they lived there, but her father told her that if they did they'd never be able to enjoy it. She was told that people from New York never did the fun things her family got to do, like go to Broadway shows or do the Statue of Liberty tour. People in New York didn't have any money. It had to be a lie, Lis thought. It was one of those things, like how her father would complain about city parking, but clearly there had to be a way to get spots. How else did all the cars get there before her father did?

Moving to New York was an aspiration; acting was a means. She learned that she was good at it in middle school. She went to theater camp, and graduated from a local performing arts high school with honors. Her college took her on scholarship, and her parents paid the remainder of what financial aid didn't cover. It wasn't a free ride, but it was one she wouldn't face the conse-quences of until much later when she established a payment plan with her loan servicer. Compared to the sacrifices others had to make, it was manageable.

Orientation was extravagant. The school plotted an entire month of get-togethers and activities for incoming freshmen, assuming the slots open for early move-in would be gobbled up quickly and students would be spending the latter half of the summer there. Tyler and Madison had already been living at the dorms for two weeks when Lis arrived. She'd met Madison and Silvia on a Facebook group for incoming freshmen, and they'd gotten along enough to choose each other as roommates. Tyler made several appearances on Madison's social media pages. She clicked through page after page of photos in which they posed in costumes from school musicals, did outdoor activities like hiking and kayaking, posed stiffly in prom attire, and celebratorily in grad robes. The most recent ones saw them standing on steps of famous New York landmarks together—the Met, the Statue of Liberty, Katz's Delicatessen (at which they did not eat, but rather stood outside of for a picture). His name was tagged everywhere, and its simplicity and its length fit nicely with captions like "Class of '14!" and "We'll have what she's having!"

Lis thought Tyler was gay, based on the photos, but when she met him she questioned herself; he was too nice. One day soon after move-in, when she and Madison were alone and she was feeling free and bold, the new girl in New York City, she asked flatly, "Is Tyler gay?" Madison, who had been unpacking many pairs of leggings for her upcoming daily dance classes said, "No, and believe me, *I'd* know. I've always told him I'd be supportive and he insists there's nothing to tell me. He *knows* I'd be his surrogate if he needed one." Madison's answer did not actually make Lis much more sure, but straight men who were mistaken for gay were her favorite. All her life, the boys and idols she had crushes on were called faggots by jackasses in school. This endeared them to her. Before they dated, Lis and Tyler were friends. He was a very nice boy, and though not religious, he had an eerie evangelical cast to him. She reminded him of kids she'd grown up with who had pastors for dads. When Madison and Lis got home and into bed after the drag show, Lis was haunted by visions of Tyler as she fell asleep.

The following morning, Lis woke up in the pine lean-to of her bottom bunk to find that she couldn't sense Madison's feverish oblong of energy above her, nor could she see a lump across the room in Silvia's bunk. Lis got up, realizing the time. It was one PM. As she sat up, a rush of blood sank into her underwear, and she jolted out of bed before she could stain the sheet. She wondered if this explained her irritability last night. Once she started bleeding, her moods evened right out, but in the days leading up she was a nightmare. She knew she'd woken up just in time to prevent a sheet-ruining catastrophe, but her pajamas were in danger, so she quickly hop-stepped over the wrinkled pantyhose on the floor and rushed to the toilet. After cleaning up, she checked her face in the mirror. She'd done a bad job scrubbing the mascara out of her eyes when she got home, and now she was bloodshot. She washed, feeling all the new bumps on her face from the hormone rush. Disappointing; she'd been having a run of good skin lately.

She went to the kitchenette, and noticed Trevor in a sad and stinking state on the couch. His shoes and jacket were off and blanket was over him, which did not seem to be his own doing. The sound of her movement woke him, and he opened his eyes like a baby, croaking awake. Pitifully, he greeted her. "Hi honey...."

"Good morning sweet pea."

"And how are you?"

"Holding up."

Trevor sat up. He didn't gag, showing the strength of his constitution. He asked for coffee.

"You don't want water? Coffee's going to dehydrate you."

"I think I'd rather be dry and alive."

He got up to sit at the kitchen island. Lis had once been told that when they were designing the dorms, they could have put in a table and chairs, or a couch. Without the couches, these wouldn't have looked like real apartments, but with them, families were more likely to feel good about the boarding costs. The kitchen island completed the picture of a real apartment, despite the lack of an oven and the two-burner electric hotplate set in the counter for a stove. Lis asked Trevor where everyone was.

"Oh yeah, Silvia is at auditions for the winter show, she's going for a solo in *The Nutcracker*."

"She's *auditioning* today?" Looking at Trevor, Lis could only imagine what shape Silvia was in.

"I know, don't you love that crazy bitch?"

Lis began to work the Keurig that Madison had brought with her from home when the moved in. It was huge and bad for the environment, but they were all grateful for it.

"What about Madison?"

"Uh, she's doing some group project thing in the library. Or she had to go grocery shopping. One of those."

Just then, Lis got a low cramp. She stopped still, holding an empty Keurig pod. Trevor wasn't phased, he'd seen it all before. He asked if she had plans for the day, which she both did and didn't. Weekends were days that Tyler expected they'd spend together, though he never actually reached out to make plans. They saw each other every day, either in class or in the halls, and he often made a vague suggestion about going to a coffee shop or some other place where they could sit and talk on the weekends. He had few ideas for dates. Now that they had the scene work to do, he threw offers to get extra rehearsal time as well. Lis wanted fancier dates; museums, maybe clubs; things that took advantage of the city, not things they could do anywhere. Then again, Tyler's dates were easy and guaranteed she'd be home not long after dark. Lis told Trevor she could probably text Tyler and do some scene work or something. Trevor *hmmed* and began to drink his coffee.

"So.... I couldn't help but notice last night, you were talking to a cute someone at the bar?"

Lis was surprised that Trevor had noticed.

"You saw?"

"I did, and I know Madison did too, but god bless her I don't think she thought twice about it. For all she knew that place was fifty shades of faggot and there was no reason to be suspicious."

"Suspicious?"

"Well *I'm* not suspicious; that's a bad way to put it. And you don't seem nervous. And anyway, I'm not judgemental. *And* I think monogamy is a scam, so."

"So what?"

Trevor leaned in over his coffee, the scent from his pores

potent and flammable. "Look, all I'm saying, is that if you had a secret, it would be safe with me." Trevor made his face straight and serious, and paused for effect. "And if you wanted to go to another show, I'll take you. I just didn't think you'd enjoy them that much."

"Why not?"

"I don't know, I thought you might be freaked out or something, but maybe I was getting you confused with Madison."

Lis bristled at being compared to Madison, but let it go, because Trevor's offer of escort was more precious to Lis. It was an invitation, an arm extended to formalize a friendship she didn't realize had been forged until this moment. This was one of those moments where if she made the right decision, the life she'd have after her degree would assume a new shape, a butterfly choice. That hypothetical, rapidly encroaching life was forming its strictures just outside of her line of sight, waiting for the day when she would fit into it. Thinking of the feeling she felt at that bar, the insecurity and discomfort that, in her waking hours, felt more acutely like a kind of self-loathing, she thought that maybe Trevor was her angel. This person in front of her could be the one to show her in, make her feel like she belonged in the place that she wanted to belong. And maybe, if she accepted his offer to do that, she would expand like a gas to fill the space given to her.

"When's the next one?"

2017

It was pitiful but true that Ty hadn't been with anyone since Nat. He didn't think it was for lack of trying, and he worried that what had happened years ago had permanently damaged his romantic capabilities. He was further worried that something in him atrophied, and the fear of being alone haunted him every day, though he was good enough at distracting himself with work and shows and friends to feel like his head was above water. He did not like dating apps, he was scared of them. He preferred to date people he already knew, but he didn't meet new people often. Lita had been the last new person he'd met in the past year, but she quickly got involved with Silvia and after that Ty knew he would never have a chance.

Max once told him that he'd changed since Nat. They were finishing up a takeout dinner last winter when the subject came up; this was when they had become aware that their old roommate was on his way out, and before resorting to strangers, they considered which of their friends needed housing. Nat was looking for a place to live after his graduation, prompting Ty to wonder how terrible of an idea it might be to live with someone he fucked around once upon a time. "Nat's parents give him money, so it should be fine," he'd said; the prospect of a financially comfortable roommate helped smooth a lot of things over. Max was not opposed to the idea, but a little perturbed. She listened to his explanation for why this was a good idea, and it wasn't that she didn't believe it was, but rather that she questioned how welcome Nat would actually be in the apartment. As a friend to both of them, she tried to tease Ty into dealing with his emotions. "You know, the average person doesn't invite an ex to come live in their apartment."

"We never dated." After a thought, he asked, "Wait, by average, do you mean straight?"

She raised an eyebrow. "Aren't you 'straight'?"

"Sort of, but I'm not *average* straight."

"Oh, you sad man."

"Hello?"

"Listen to you, bi-curious!"

"Alright first of all, fuck off, and second of all, who said I was opening up anything?"

"You used to be pretty average straight if I remember correctly."

"Well, maybe you don't remember correctly."

"Uh-huh. Well, I *would* like a roommate with money, and Nat's cute, so go ahead and send the text if you want."

"I thought you might make the offer."

"Wrong." She smiled and went back to work on her summer roll, leaving Ty to type up a text. He deleted their message exchange to clear out his phone on a regular basis, but his computer did this mean thing where he could delete the thread as many times as he wanted, but on sending a new message, the full history of their communication via text came back like a boomerang. Ty had few occasions to send Nat a message, and most of the ones from the past year had been *we're here, Silvia asked if you're on the train.* In order to offer Nat a room, he had to look at those dry notifications and know that if he scrolled up a bit he'd find a chunk of grey pleading messages, cringe-inducing flirt texts, and then finally the first message Nat had ever sent him: *its Lis :3.*

In the short time Nat had been living with them, he paid his share of the rent on time, bought paper towels and toilet paper when it was his turn, and did his dishes. Max was obsessed with these qualities, Ty would not praise someone for the bare minimum. He couldn't help but feel that Nat's goodness as a roommate was a cover. For Ty, assuming the worst in Nat was a defense mechanism gone rogue. He'd been burned once, and granted, that was a long time ago, but he was nothing if not paranoid. Ty intentionally excluded Nat from even the most peripheral of roles in the remainder of his adult life. He and Nat were roommates, not friends. The distinction was important, even if Nat was beloved by the people Ty held most dear. Ty had other priorities; securing a good job, a good apartment, good friends, and finding a partner: he'd accomplished three-quarters of these goals, and he was happy. Very happy, very satisfied, no reasons to complain. His loneliness was not killing him, he told himself, it was simply a side effect of getting "established." He just didn't have the time for dating. He used to, but he didn't know where all that time had gone.

The three of them living together worked well, for the most part. The newly outness of Nat meant that he often opened his mouth to reveal irritating misconceptions, and Ty sometimes found himself wishing there was a charm school for baby trannies. The difficulty in bearing with it was that in a broader sense, Nat's ideals were the same as his, so the things Nat sometimes said were not evident of some kind of insidious secret alt-right conservatism, but rather sticky things from closeted life. Things like not realizing the transphobia inherent to the concept of gendered socialization, or only understanding the misogyny he grew up with as the unique domain of female-assigned people. He was in the process of getting to where Ty was now, which served as a reminder to Ty that he had been Nat once; some could bear with this reminder more gracefully than others. Nat thought that there was a neat divide between trans men and women, where trans women were very visible and got magazine covers and media attention—"but obviously that's not always a *good* thing," he was quick to add—and trans men were ignored and surfaced on TV occasionally as pale radar blips. This was not necessarily untrue, but Nat thought of visibility in very basic terms. He thought it was like math: If cis people cannot see you or understand you, how can you exist? These ignorances were picked up along the way of his adolescence, especially during his teenage and early college years, around the same time that Taylor Swift decided to rebrand herself as a feminist. Nat's words reeked of white feminism and perpetual bedroom Tumblr-scrolling, and though he showed signs of genuine humiliation once made aware of these errors, Ty hated to watch Lita and Max's faces as they took on the burden of setting him straight when nearly the same words had been used on them like weapons. What had Nat done to earn either of their generosities? Ty himself had gone through this, but he'd learned how to act right on his own, without help.

If there was a trans baby boom, Nat was part of it. He saw their world in simple terms; the genderbread man, binaries made of the most binary-defying concepts, poor critical thinking skills, a flag for everything. Ty knew that if it weren't for the company Nat kept, he could expect to see him on the internet squawking at any proudly-slurring queer who dared hold two thoughts in their head at once. There had been one nightmarish evening at home after one of Max's shows when Nat would not shut up about how offended he'd been by the lesbian with the trans boyfriend. "I just don't know how he deals with that, she's basically going around telling people she thinks he's a woman." The lesbian in question was not strictly a woman themself, but the shit was already deep and Ty didn't have a paddle. Max said: "that's their relationship and it's not our business." Nat said, "yeah, I'm just *saying*, I feel bad for him." Ty knew the man in question, and knew based on several envy-inducing details that he did *not* need anyone to feel bad for him. What proceeded was a noticeably exasperated Max in half-drag trying to explain the concept of nuance to a vodka-steeped twink. Ty mostly held his tongue, but when sufficiently irritated he cut in to make little objections, eventually getting irritated enough to say in a slightly too-severe voice, "you not getting it makes no fucking difference." He hoped this would end the conversation, and Max and Nat did look at him for a few beats, but then they continued to go over the problem like Ty was the wind. At one point, Nat said something catty about how Ty had dated a few lesbians in his time. He must have heard this from Max, since Ty would never share the details of his romantic history with Nat.

"Well," he replied, "historically, dating straight girls goes pretty poorly for me."

Nat quieted. For a moment, Ty regretted his words, as Nat's face gave away real pain. Max tried to keep the silence from going on too long and quickly began a new train of thought; Ty was tired, and he didn't care to stay awake longer to find out whether Nat could develop a brain. He washed his face and locked himself in his bedroom without another word.

Ty remembered when Nat told him about all the vlogs he used to watch. These were mostly guys who'd transitioned around the same time Ty did, and he was familiar with a few of them, but he was never interested in their videos, possibly because Ty was already out whereas Nat needed those videos to live vicariously under the guise of being a very good ally. Ty felt there was something cowardly to that, like rehearsing something difficult until you felt ready instead of just doing it. After they fell out, Ty revisited those vlogs, and ended up annoyed and tired. He was sure that some of these guys were cool to hang out with, but the "community" of trans guy Youtubers generally reminded him too much of mid-twenties youth pastors. It was the way they repeated the same lessons over and over, every video starting with them greeting the audience to let them know he was here to "correct misconceptions." Correcting misconceptions was a noble pursuit, but it left little time to form any new conceptions, so these videos were repetitive. It seemed that everyone needed to make at least one video about starting T, one about sexuality, one about top surgery (and the concurrent or consequent top surgery reveal, which nine times out of ten was filmed in the same Florida surgeon's office that Ty saw in his nightmares), one about sex, and one about how though they were wracked with horrible dysphoria they thought bottom surgery was a terrible idea. It wouldn't be so bad if there were any kind of dialogue between these people, but they all had the exact same opinions. Well, there was a one vlogger, not one of Nat's fixations but a new one, who'd just started within the last year or so whose thoughts did differ, but in the sense that he was as repulsed by difference as any white man and reduced himself and others to a list of pathologized DSM criteria. Though this was one man, child really, since he was only eighteen, his very loud audience of frothing teenagers killed Ty's hopes that things would ever progress. He often wished he had more friends like him, but struggled to stomach the behavior of the ones most visible online. His greatest fear was that he would live his whole life and trannies would just have the same argument over and over again, talking with their mouths full of their own tails.

5

2015

On Lis's first date with Tyler, she wore purple lipstick. It was a shade called "Temptation" that looked like stepped-on blueberries, She'd been wearing it since high school, a stylistic choice embedded by the fact that her mother hated it—not because it was ugly, but because it was "from the eighties." *Then why do they still make it?* Lis had asked. *People do lots of stupid things for too long for no reason,* was the answer. Anyway, it became Lis's favorite. It looked good against her skin and the black clothes she wore. When she was thirteen, auditioning for her local performing arts high school, she was told to wear black. Actors needed to slip into character at any moment; black clothes rendered them void and waiting. Lis, already addicted to being on stage, to applause, to satisfaction, was titillated again. Confirmation of the right choice, a choice of career that would ensure she'd always be impossibly glamorous, as long as she played her cards right and made it. She got into that program, and wore black every day. She accumulated black skirts, tights, boots, sweaters, underwear, and accessories. Without realizing it, she'd formed her personality around the clothes that were supposed to suppress it. In New Jersey, she came across as stylish, and shopping was easy. Any colorful clothes in her closet were gifts from her mother and aunts, who assumed she didn't wear them because she didn't know how to.

Getting ready for the first date with Tyler, she'd backed up and looked in the full-length mirror on the back of the bedroom door. She liked it. She backed up further, picturing herself from farther and farther away, the way a stranger would see her from two blocks over. Would they be stunned? Frightened? Would they notice her?

On Saturday, she put the lipstick on again to go to the show with Trevor. Just the two of them. Trevor didn't know who Lis had spoken to last time by name, but he recognized his face. "He's there all the time with his little futch cohort." Trevor felt confident that he was familiar enough to get Lis a proper introduction. Lis was worried this was all for nothing. She thought she was going to come across as way too intense, that he'd be able to tell that she'd come there for him. As she was tidying her clothes and re-parting her hair, Madison came in noisily, it sounded like she was juggling her keys like a circus clown. Lis listened to the sounds of Madison putting her bag down and huffing towards the bedroom, where Lis and Trevor were stationed on the floor, each kneeling in front of a portable vanity mirror.

"I thought you had midterms to study for?" Lis had been expecting, and hoping, that Madison would be preoccupied in the library and that she might not come home until she and Trevor were already gone.

"So do you!" Madison responded.

Lis spoke lightly in an effort to sound vaguely complimentary, "Well, I guess I'm not as responsible as you!" Trevor did not speak at all.

Madison grabbed four different kinds of body scrub from her dresser drawer and made for the shower. "Anyway, I'm too stressed out to do anything right now. I just didn't realize you were going out tonight." She spoke as if she had been invited.

Trevor clapped his mirror shut and tapped Lis on the wrist. "Sweetie, we gotta book it."

And they did, straight to the newly-repaired elevator after rushing through chipper goodbyes. As soon as the dorm door was closed, Trevor's thoughts turned to Silvia, who was busy with preparations for the winter dance showcase. If they asked, Silvia likely could have made time, but the mission of the night was clandestine, and though both Lis and Trevor trusted Silvia, it seemed too complicated to draw her in.

Lis, now outside the cloud of flushed anxiety Madison carried around with her, said, "We're too mean to her."

"I know, but she's so annoying."

"Yeah, but she's not hurting anyone."

Trevor pursed his lips and sighed, then gave a conciliatory nod before saying, "In a year or something I'm sure she'll be great, but her parents gave her a complex by putting her in SAT Prep when she was twelve and she needs to get over it. Let her fail a test and see that she doesn't explode. Or get fucked, or *something.*"

Funny, thought Lis. Madison's obsession with school was not the thing Lis thought of as annoying. What Lis hated about Madison was her franticness, they way that even at baseline she could stress someone out by breathing the same air. It was a repulsion, but a guilty one.

They got to the venue early, a blessing from Trevor that gave Lis time to scan the bar for her guy. She spotted him standing in a loose gaggle with the host, Max, and a few others; it appeared to be the same group of friends who had teased him last time. Lis hadn't considered the friends, and now worried about what would happen if one of them recognized her and alerted him. Now that she'd gotten this far, she wasn't sure what to do next. Should she approach, or wait for him to notice her? She had a feeling he would remember her despite, or perhaps because of, the awkward impression she'd made last time. Alas, Trevor was impatient. He took her hand and led her over to the group in a march, under the pretense of wanting to introduce himself to the host. She was nervous, but grateful that he didn't just throw her at him as she worried he might.

After Trevor gave some impressive praise to Max, Lis's guy turned to her. "So you're back for more?"

Surprised and pleased, and a little shy to be addressed directly, she said, "Ah, yeah. I really enjoyed myself last time."

"Cool, it's good to see you again."

Lis felt, more than saw, the presence of Trevor's face not far from hers, then saw his hand stretch toward the guy like a tentacle, "*Hi*, I'm Trevor." Again, Lis was embarrassed by Trevor's forward-ness, but he *was* making this easier for her. She didn't get the guy's name last time, as he didn't give it, yet still she worried about offending him by not knowing it.

"Ty," he said while graciously accepting Trevor's handshake.

Lis knew this was an opportunity for life to overwhelm her with regret, but she resisted.

"Oh, that's delicious," said Trevor.

"Thank you?"

Fuck, she thought. She took the natural turn of the conversation to introduce herself, the pleasure of being able to tell him her name softening the embarrassment of his his having nearly the same name as the boyfriend she'd rather forget existed.

Ty smiled. "It's nice to meet the both of you." Did he really mean *both* of them, or was he only saying that to be nice and he was really happy to meet *her* specifically?

A track began to play over the bar's sound system that announced Max's official entrance to the stage. The first leg of the journey was over, she'd made a second trip out, she'd managed to properly introduce herself, and she didn't feel too bad. Thanks to the crowd, she was locked in place between Ty and Trevor for the show. The mission on one side, her guide on the other. She could stop here, she could be satisfied that this man had noticed her and remembered her for a whole two weeks. Maybe she could entertain herself thinking of the thoughts he might have had about her. And she didn't have to go as far as real cheating. She could operate with a clean conscience, go home to the dorms, maybe come back here a few times and let that be the end of the story, and then what? Be haunted by the potential of what could have been?

No, she already loved it too much. This time around, with Trevor as her only connection to real life, she actually *felt* where she was. She laughed harder, she smiled brighter, felt cozier. She thought she understood things a bit better now, and she preferred Ty's small attentions to anything she'd gotten from Tyler. She listened to his whoops and whistles at the performers from right next to him; it charmed her to know that he was cheering for people he knew and probably loved. Life in the dorms vanished from her head. Suddenly, she was out of school, post-grad. An adult in this place, here with her friends, with whom she'd been hanging around as long as anyone could remember. Unsure of how she fit, but sure that she did, she knew what she wanted to do, so when the show broke for intermission she followed Ty and his friends outside for their smoke break. Trevor followed *her* for a change, and sneakily monopolized the conversational attention of Ty's friends so that he'd be left with her on the fringes. She was touched by Trevor's willingness to be rude to Ty for her sake. It was early October cold, a ticklish sharp air that made the secondhand smoke smell better. Ty wore a leather jacket. He left it unzipped, and for the first time she saw what he looked like under something resembling natural light. He was so gorgeous. She wanted to lean on him the way she did with Tyler sometimes, to compare the sensations. She was certain Ty would feel better, but she knew she had to wait; she didn't want to spoil the whole thing by being too eager. These were her calculations, the same math she did for all interactions, but specialized for the purpose of winning someone. It was what she'd done to get Tyler.

She barely remembered what happened during the conversation, only that Trevor was entertaining, she was quiet, and Ty was perfect. She learned a handful of things about him, but didn't really remember how they came out. He was twenty-three, though she expected him to be older. He was finishing school in Brooklyn because he was from here and he got cheaper tuition from a CUNY than she would have. He studied design and had a minor, but she forgot what it was. He lived with Max and another roommate, he had a brother. He couldn't play any instruments.

The second act was even better than the first. When the crowd re-grouped at the stage, everyone from the smoke break was rosy-cheeked like a holiday card. She felt that if she were bolder she'd go home with Ty. If she wasn't still on her period, maybe that'd be a more realistic possibility. On the way out, Ty asked if he could give her his number. No one had asked for permission to give her a gift before. She passed him her phone and watched him type it in. When she got it back, his name was there with a :).

"Do you want to take mine?" she asked.

"That's okay, just text me and I'll get it."

He was giving her another choice. She could bury that phone number, but if she wanted him badly enough, she would use it. He was measuring her. Ty walked off with Max and some of their friends, and Trevor took her hand to lead her to an Uber. On the ride, she sent her name to Ty.

2017

"Do you think that perhaps you were a little, cold? One might say, a cunt?" Max said. She was trying her best to gently suggest to Ty that an apology might be in order. "Cold, yes. Cunt, very possible, but did I say anything that was incorrect?" He argued. "Well, depending on how you look at it, you called him a girl."

Ty's cheeks got warm. "I wouldn't go *that* far." Max nodded, pulling her mug of coffee off the kitchen counter to hold it close to her chest. "You know you have to let it go at some point, don't you?" It was hard for Ty to look at her. If she were anyone else, he would be offended by such a question. "I have."

"Have you?"

"He lives here, doesn't he?"

"Right, at your suggestion, if I remember correctly."

"You don't. Anyway, what's done is done, I got used, and now we're moving on. We're not friends and that works fine for both of us."

Max put her hand on his shoulder for a little caress. "Okay." Ty didn't meet her gaze, but he knew that the look she was giving him was not one of conviction. They had woken up late after the last show; there was stray weed spilled on the coffee table that gave him an idea of how Max and Nat's charm school session had gone. He vaguely remembered waking up in the middle of the night to hear them chatting and smoking, which made him feel like a child sent to bed early during a grown-up party. He swept the stray bits into his palm and tossed them before sitting and putting his feet on the table. "You pig," Max said, before sitting in the chair beside him. "I don't know why I'm getting so comfortable, I have work to do" she said. Just then, Nat emerged from his room, hungover. Max gave him a good morning greeting and watched him shuffle to the coffee maker. He reached for the handle, then stopped himself and instead ran the tap to chug a big glass of water. Then he resumed the motions of making his coffee. All this was done in silence, with his back to the sofa. Ty knew that if he left, Max and Nat would likely have the other side of the conversation he'd just been having with her. That is, if they hadn't already discussed it last night. Ty sometimes found himself jealous of the way Max and Nat had become so close. He was glad that at least one person in the apartment could tolerate Nat, but he had begun to feel left out. This was probably how their old roommate used to feel. Ty didn't want to be the new straight man.

Max turned to Ty, "do you need the living room for anything important today?" She asked.

Given that she was already moving the furniture, he said, "Uh, I guess not."

"Good, we're gonna move some furniture around so I can show Nat a few things."

Ty wasn't sure if he wanted to know, but he asked anyway, "things?"

Instead of letting Max reply, Nat spoke up to address Ty directly, "I'm doing the open set next week."

"Oh." The open set was an opportunity for new drag artists to take the stage, provided that their number was under four minutes and didn't involve any mess. Max did this at her shows every few months, and it was usually a cute way to get people in the door. A few exceptional artists had had their debut at Max's, and it was no coincidence that these were people who'd gotten some pointers from Max beforehand, the same special attention Nat was apparently getting now. Ty thought of all the places he could go that day to make himself scarce. He didn't want to listen to Max mothering Nat anymore. He finished his coffee and went to dress in his room. Once he had pants on, he opened the window and climbed out onto the fire escape. He wished he had a cigarette, but he'd managed to stay off of them for longer than he ever had before, and with each day that passed on this streak, the pressure to keep it going increased. The crack in the alley was spreading. New spidery tendrils had sprung from it; maybe the humidity had something to do with it. One of his upstairs neighbors had thrown some trash out of her window and missed the recycling cans the landlord kept back there. Ty imagined that every time she dropped something, a new crack broke through the concrete.

One of Ty's habits was taking stock of his friendships. He listed all the people he kept in his life, how he thought they thought of him, where he stood with them. The list was smaller every year, but the people he liked the most remained present. Lita, Silvia, Max. Though he knew that his friends had boundless patience, he worried that with how much they liked Nat, his bitterness would eventually put a strain on his relationships with them. Having Nat live with him and Max was partially a safeguard against this. It was a show of good faith, perhaps excessively so. Keeping Nat close was a way to prove that he was capable of moving on, but, as Max had noticed, it wasn't Nat pulling up hurdles. It was painfully clear that his friends had all had enough of Ty's refusal to forget the events of 2015. Ty had too, yet that resentment kept something in him alive.

Looking down the fire escape, he wondered if he could leave the apartment out the back, so as to get away without giving Nat the satisfaction of knowing he'd been driven out. It was a stupid idea though, the ladder at the bottom would probably break off if he tried to use it. He watched a stray cat eat a dandelion out of the cement canyon. Eventually, he decided to call his pharmacy for something to do. It wasn't the same as leaving the apartment, but it was a guaranteed waste of forty minutes, and he needed a distraction.

6

When walking along the halls between classes, Lis often worried that an imperfection in the tile or the carpet would trip her. It was unnecessary to look up from her phone while navigating, as the building was fairly small and she knew her way around, but in the last week, she'd felt remarkably unsteady, to the point of feeling an urge to grab onto the hall rails for balance. She wondered if she was developing vertigo, but not once did she ever feel truly dizzy. She stared at her feet more than usual, scanning for suspicious activity. Lis had always felt that she was at risk of a sudden attack of clumsiness, but it seemed to be getting worse. This might have made her more upset, but her troubles were soothed by her growing friendship with Ty.

Lis texted Ty every day. Though it seemed like they were having hours long conversations, it was mostly flirting with tiny bursts of information here and there. She told him about how she'd been born in Jersey but always loved the city, he told her about how Staten Island, where he was born, was dead grass and mean dogs, and Bay Ridge, where he was raised, was green grass and mean people. He told her about how he'd met Max shortly before she'd dropped out of their design program, which he was due to finish. She told him about how Trevor would live in her dorm if it was co-ed. He asked her if she preferred his home bar to other places she could spend a Saturday night, she told him that there was no place she'd rather be.

Lis went somewhere when she was texting Ty. The truth was usually that she was in her bed or between classes, but to her, it felt like she was hidden in another plane of existence when talking to him, safe from the rest of the world. Ever since she'd gotten his number, her video-binging habit had withered. When she wasn't texting Ty, she was consumed by an anxiety that she could not place. It must have been guilt, even though she didn't really feel bad for Tyler, which only made made her more nervous. She must really be a callous person to have no regard for the boyfriend she was growing tired of. It would have been better to cut him loose now that she knew her heart was else-where, but she was attached to him in the way that one might be to a utility knife. Their scene work was only getting more tiresome, and they rehearsed less and less frequently. Tyler had finally gotten off book, which meant that he now looked her in the eyes while they were performing, so she did her best to make excuses for why she wouldn't be able to run lines with him.

When Tyler announced that his dorm-mates had all been cast in the same one-act play written for someone else's final project, Lis realized that he'd been waiting for an opening to invite her over, and seemed to expect that she'd been waiting for an invi-tation. The most they'd done in the time they'd been together was make out. Lis was ambivalent about losing her virginity. She kept up a feminist perspective that it was no big deal, it wasn't really a loss, and it would just happen when it happened. Now, it seemed like signals were turning on to say, "okay, here." Tyler was handsome, they'd been together long enough, and he was nice, so it'd be fine. Easy.

She didn't want to go over before the roommates left. It embarrassed her to think about them leaving, cracking jokes about the two of them on the way out, knowing what she (who had never been to their dorm before) was in for. She wondered if Tyler jerked off in the shared bedroom.

He lived on the seventh floor; she was panting when she got in, since the elevator had broken down again. To Tyler, it looked like she was eager. They kissed in the living room, but being on the couch that had been used by other students for years made her uneasy. The dorm mattresses might be old too, but at least Tyler's own sheets were on them. She regretted moving them to the bedroom though, since the beds of the roommates made her feel like they weren't alone, and it smelled like the windows hadn't been opened in months. Sure, it was getting colder out, but in her dorm they still opened them to let the air circulate.

Lis tried to get excited, but she had low expectations. She knew that this might hurt, and it was unlikely she'd come. Her odds were slightly increased since she'd been masturbating successfully since puberty started and knew how to touch herself, but she had little confidence in Tyler figuring out what to do. She realized that she didn't know if he'd done this before, but she assumed he hadn't. He did not use his hands on her at all, except to spread her legs. She took off her own clothes. She didn't realize that she'd be naked. In her imaginings, she kept a shirt and skirt on, being in too much of a hurry to get started. But fore-play seemed to last forever, and Tyler made a show of taking off a piece of his clothing and watching her remove its counterpart from her body. He kissed her with eyes closed while putting the condom on, and not being able to watch him do it made her worry that he hadn't done it right. She wanted to look down and check, but when he broke the kiss, he was already in her. It didn't hurt, but it did feel too overwhelming to feel good. She couldn't tell if he felt big because she'd never done this before, or if he actually was big. He was inconsistent with his thrusts. It seemed like he'd gotten the advice that he should provide a variety of sensations, but he switched tempo so fast that it felt like being fucked by a paint mixer. If he was waiting for her to tell him what felt good, it wasn't clear when he wanted her to speak. She made noises that came out sounding confused, more due to the motion than anything, but he was encouraged by them, and after about seven minutes it was clear he wasn't going to last much longer. He closed his eyes and put his head back, giving Lis a moment to move her hand and stroke herself, hoping to get something out of the experience. It felt much better, the thrusts felt more productive and she was able to relax. Tyler opened his eyes again though, and her hand snapped away from force of habit, like she'd been caught jerking off. Tyler looked a bit pitiful; his expression was aiming for what, awe? But instead he looked pleading.

"Can I?"

"Yeah."

And he did, for about half a minute. He pitched himself over her while catching his breath, and Lis squirmed, worried that he would get soft and the condom would leak. He pulled out of her, making little grimacing noises as he did. Lis felt like she'd just watched him shit himself.

"I'm just going to go to the bathroom real quick."

Tyler mumbled something disappointed-sounding in answer.

She escaped. She didn't want to watch him while his breathing returned to normal. She especially didn't want to be asked any questions. Her body was confused. She deliberated getting herself off in the bathroom, but the plumbing fixtures and shampoo bottles that looked like evil twins of the ones in her dorm depressed her. She ran cold water in the sink, splashed some on her face, and wiped herself down with toilet paper. She wanted a shower, and wondered how soon she could leave. In hindsight, she should have tried to time this closer to when the roommates were coming back. She could have used them as an excuse, leaving Tyler with no time to talk or go again. She worried he might ask if she finished and offer to "help." Stupid, she hadn't thought to fake it.

Her clothes were still in Tyler's room. When she went back in, she noticed they were under him, being sweated on. Tyler himself looked nearly asleep, but then he turned his head and smiled at her, gesturing for her to come in and cuddle. She did. The feeling of his skin on hers would be fine if he were dry, but he'd worked up such a dampness when all she wanted to do was shower, or at least open a window. He still had cum stuck to him. She spent eleven minutes laying there out of obligation, and then she made an excuse that she ought to get back before anyone noticed what was up. Tyler lightly pleaded with her to stay, but smirked through it, enjoying the mischief of being young and getting away with this, as if they were back in someone's parents' house. The fun he was having made her sick.

She ran up to her own dorm. The keys seemed to know how badly she needed to get in, because they didn't fumble around like they usually did. Silvia and Trevor were inside. Outside, it was less cold and she had no coat on—it was obvious she'd come from somewhere else in the dorms. She expected an insinuating "ooh" when they saw the state she was in, but they either didn't care or Lis looked awful, because they said nothing but "hi" and left her unmolested while she grabbed pajamas and a fresh towel to shower. She used every fancy product she had; the cucumber scrub, the glittering body wash, the silky soap foam. She must have used three detergents and a dozen fragrance extracts in the thirty-five minutes she stood under the water. She knew better than to put soaps inside her, but still, she took two of her fingers and swabbed to remove anything that might be there. There was nothing but her own discharge, as she expected, but the action made her feel relieved. There were two other kinds of relief on her mind: the sex being over in the sense she wasn't in Tyler's embrace anymore, and the relief that it was an experience to cross off her to-do list. She wasn't a virgin anymore, no one could say she was. If she was going to regret it, she couldn't tell yet, and she expected to be like all the other non-virgins she knew who all agreed that their first time was a nightmare.

For as rattled as she felt, she would have expected her breathing to be irregular, but she appeared calm in body, and the bathroom was full of steam and smell. She combed through wet hair and put herself in pajamas, and thought it was good that Madison wasn't home. Clean and fresh, she went to the bedroom and piled herself heavily with blankets, then put in her head-phones and queued up several videos to watch, nearly a week's worth of life updates. A guy in the Bay Area who she followed closely had been told his BMI was too high for top surgery, so he was now considering various diets; another in Iowa was in the process of defending his PhD dissertation; one in Montreal had just broken up with his partner, also well-known in the FTM vlogging community; that partner had conspicuously not uploaded a video about the breakup and now appeared to be courting a girl he'd gone to school with. She spent a long time watching these videos, going to the same place she went to when she talked to Ty. As if he knew she needed him, a notification appeared at the top of her phone, interrupting someone's fourth video on phalloplasty. He'd sent her a photo of the view from his fire escape, a big flaming sunset backlighting the concrete building across from the back of his apartment. A lacy stream of smoke in the corner of the frame explained why he was sitting out there in the cold. There was no message attached. She wrote back, *wish I was there.* A few moments later, a gray bubble said: *we can make that happen.*

2017

Max had not asked Ty to bring anything, which was unusual. The last time this had happened was when she'd had a boyfriend for a few weeks the previous year, one who briefly acted as Ty's replacement before deciding that the life of a drag boyfriend was not for him. Ty tried to enjoy the comfort of being unbur-dened as he got ready for the show at Lita's apartment with her and Silvia. For him, getting ready meant pulling together an outfit from his closet which was slowly becoming imbalanced; weighted in favor of work clothes rather than what he used to consider his "normal" clothes. He thought about changing out some of his piercings, but it was due to be a hot night, and he didn't like wearing anything heavy in his septum when the weather was like this. He watched Silvia apply something red to her lips, wipe it off, and then apply the same color a second time. It was rare to see her second-guess herself. Lita was already done, and she busied herself with pushing knick-knacks around on her bookshelf while chatting with Ty.

"Should we pregame?" She asked. "It's going to be crowded at the bar."

Silvia piped up, "Maybe after I finish my eyeliner, but we should probably head out soon."

"I could go for a shot, honestly," said Ty. He'd been feeling edgy all day, like a maladjusted preschooler. If one annoying thing happened to him he could blow, which was unusual. He was an irritable person, but he usually felt much more in control of himself. It had to be hormones. He'd been told that the reason it was taking so long to get a new T prescription had something to do with his insurance, which didn't make sense to him since his insurance had never covered the drug anyway. But, because of changes to clinic policy, they now had to try to bill insurance for every prescription renewal before allowing patients the sliding scale fee. He probably could have afforded the $90 out of pocket cost, but if he did it once, he would be expected to do so again next time, and he couldn't deal with a $90 recurring charge, especially when the cost tended to go up every year at unpredictable rates. He hated the term "mood swing." It made him feel stupid.

Lita poured vodka shots for the three of them, leaving Silvia's next to her vanity mirror for when she was ready. Lita looked soft, like she wanted to stroke Silvia's hair or pat her hand, but Silvia was so focused on her makeup that she seemed entirely shut off from the world. Lita passed Ty his glass. "Alright, here's to the baby boom." She said this every time Max did an open set, an homage to the ever-inflating percentage of performers were fellow patients at Ty (and Lita's) clinic. People were coming out all over the place; a good thing to be sure, though Ty was wary of meeting the newcomers. He would have loved to be more of a role model, but he avoided people under 22 in the same way he avoided children under 12, including his nieces. When Silvia announced that she was done, she called a car.

At the bar, Lita hustled to get more drinks. "Is she okay?" He asked Silvia. He worried about Lita's alcohol intake. If she drank more than she smoked, that was a bad sign. Silvia looked between Ty and her girlfriend and shrugged. "I think so, is she acting strange to you?" Ty shook his head. "I don't know, just wanted to be sure." He didn't like seeing cracks between them. The two of them made their way to a table to sit and wait until the show started. It was packed, and Ty ended up standing next to Silvia's chair in order to make way for the troops of people who had come out for the night's guest performers. Max had not emerged yet, but Ty could catch glimpses of her behind the curtain wearing her orange catsuit. Usually Ty was called on to bring the tights she wore underneath and the black wig that went with it, but that night, Nat had relieved him of that responsibility. He could see a few flashes of Nat behind the curtain as well, particularly his hair, which was out and blond. Ty found himself questioning Nat's choice to wear his own hair on his first night in drag, but then caught himself. Who was he to judge?

Lita finally made it to their table, dropping drinks in front of each of them. Since she'd gone to the bar alone, one of the drinks had to be held in the valley of her bra, and some had spilled onto her sternum. "Fuck, sorry, this one was yours." She placed the glass in front of Ty. "No need to apologize, I should have offered to help you, I didn't know you were getting one for all of us."

"Well, it seemed like the thing to do. You'll thank me later."

"What does that mean?"

"Oh, just that I saw some behind the scenes videos."

Ty smirked, "oh, that bad, huh?"

Lita smiled back. "Sure, we'll say that." An odd response, but Ty figured the shot from earlier was already working on her. After they chatted at the table for a few minutes, Max's entrance music began to play. She took the mic and gave her usual introductory spiel.

"Thank you all so much for coming tonight! If you haven't been here before, which seems likely from looking at you, I'm Max, and this is where I usually exorcise my night terrors with friends, but not tonight! Tonight, we have a whole crop of brand new baby drag virgins for you—and I expect you all to behave for them, yes?" Max led the audience through a brief demo to explain how to tip performers, a routine she'd established long ago to prevent groping incidents. It had helped tremendously, but she kept a well-built friend on standby just in case. The first act was a baby queen who had shocking dance ability, but she either didn't memorize her music, or just got nervous and forgot the words. A forgivable mistake. The second act was similar in give-and-take; a stunning beauty with utterly no stage presence. After these two, a senior performer took the stage. Max broke up the show like this just in case the newbies didn't hold the audience's attention. As much faith as she had in them, she still needed the show to have at least a guaranteed 30% success rate. It was an act of caution, but not usually necessary. Apart from the odd hyper-critical audience member, most people loudly, hoarsely championed their friends. For many people, to get up on stage was the culmination of many daydreams and defeated insecurities, and in large part thanks to Max's good hosting, the crowd was primed to receive each performer with enthusiasm.

"Well, everyone. Before I send you all into a little intermission," Max said, after a few more numbers. "We have our very last performer for this set. Don't cry, intermission is only ten minutes, allegedly! Okay, I know I'm not supposed to show bias, but I have to break my own rule here, because I have to tell you I'm especially excited for this next act." She said this every time she had a personally-trained performer come on. Rarely did she let them close an act, though. "This next performer wants you to know that he likes to confuse people. And that's all he wrote for me, a true Gemini. Please welcome to the stage, *NANCY BOY!*"

If Ty's eyes rolled any further back in his head, he would have lost them. Then, chords of a familiar song played through the bar's sound system. He didn't know Nat liked this album.

Nat had always said he wasn't a dancer; it seemed that he was also a liar. But in fairness, what Nat was doing wasn't dancing so much as it was fucking the floor. The quantity of confidence he emitted was improbable—first time performers weren't supposed to be like this. Then again, Nat was an actor, and an actor without work was an actor nonetheless. He'd been on stages before, and along the way had learned how to use them. Ty could feel Lita looking at him under her eyelashes. This was what she'd gotten him the drink for. He felt a horrifying stirring in his stomach while watching Nat, and with every sip of his drink, he felt thoughts come to him unbidden, like feral woodpeckers. Nat worked the audience, walking up and down the aisles in rhythm with the song he may or may not have known was one of Ty's recent favorites. No, he couldn't have known, Ty always listened to his music with headphones in. It just had to be something they had in common. As Nat approached, Ty's arm floated up with a dollar in his hand. He always tipped every performer, and almost out of spite, he wouldn't let Nat break that habit. But then Nat's hand grazed his when he grabbed the bill, and Ty's hips seized. He hoped no one noticed what was happening to him. He wished that the desire for Nat to come back and touch him again would go away; thankfully, Nat was back on the stage to finish the song, and after a few minutes, he was free. Before Max had even finished her first act send off, Ty was rushing to the bathroom for some peace. He managed to get there before the line did.

As far as he could tell in the dim blue light of the bathroom, there was nothing on his face to suggest how desperate his insides felt. In fact, to his surprise, he saw himself in the mirror and felt handsome. It was like he'd grown a new feature that he especially liked; generally, looking in mirrors never made him feel much of anything. His hand drifted to the fly of his pants for a moment before he drew it back, feeling pathetic.

On returning to the table after running some cold water on his wrists, Nat was standing and chatting with Lita and Silvia.

"So the stuff I sent you worked, then?" Silvia asked. Of course. Max could teach stage presence, but there wasn't a dancing bone in her body. Silvia, on the other hand, was to be held responsible for what Nat had just done, and that must have been how Lita knew what Ty would see; how she knew it would affect him the way it did was another story.

"I mean, hopefully I didn't get a UTI from the floor, but yeah I think it worked. Did people like it?"

"Oh, people liked it." Lita looked from Nat to Ty. "What did you think?" As much as Ty loved Lita, he wished she didn't have so much fun teasing him. To take too long to answer would be as bad as just giving Nat a compliment, so he quickly deadpanned, "It's a good song."

Nat was not surprised at Ty's avoidance of the question. "Thanks," he said, "it's one of my favorites."

7

Lis was eager for another drag show. She needed it like a ritual, like how in the bible women had to bathe in a certain river to get over their periods. The sex with Tyler hadn't made her feel dirty, but it *had* made her feel embarrassed. She was continuing to find ways of getting out of excess time with him. Thankfully, mid-terms were coming, so whenever he wanted to hang out, she said she had to study and instead talked shit with Trevor, texted Ty, or binged transition vlogs when she was alone. Lately Ty had been sending her pictures of latte art he made at work; a bear, a swan, a raised middle finger that he sent when they were playfully teasing each other. These texts were a lot like what she would do with boys in high school, with the crushes that never grew into anything more. In the few shows she'd been able to go to since they were properly introduced (Lis and Trevor agreed that having Lis and Silvia at the bar together would increase the risk of blowing cover, and as such, whenever Silvia had a free night and wanted to go, Lis stayed home with Madison), the air between them was intense, almost more than she could stand. To be near him was exhilarating, and terrifying. Ty was a world of possibility, one she might not be ready for. At any moment they were together, one of them might lean in closer than usual, bodies might get integrated, and Lis would be someone she wasn't sure she could be.

It was Halloween, and Lis was getting her makeup on with Trevor. This was a night Silvia would have loved to come, but she was trapped in a cruelly-scheduled rehearsal. Part of Lis had hoped that Silvia would be able to make it, thus prohibiting her from the bar according to the rules of her and Trevor's scheme, as she was struggling to come up with an excuse that would convince Tyler nothing was wrong. She could have just skipped a show and resigned to a night at some bad party with Tyler, but the thought of missing out made her itch. She told Tyler it was just too cold and her anemia was acting up. Remarkably, Tyler showed no signs of suspicion, but then he would only have noticed Lis's frequent outings if he spent any time on her floor, and he generally avoided Trevor. The careful sneaking was truly more to prevent Madison from finding out. Luckily, she was studying, spending hours away from the dorms in the library. Trevor claimed that Halloween and Madison's scarcity were what made autumn his favorite season; Lis felt obligated to scold him due to her pity for Madison's imprisonment within herself. This is what they were discussing while getting ready for Max's show.

"She's nosy and *annoying*, and no, you're right, those aren't the worst things a person can be, but like, I used to just be irritated by her but honestly? She's been pissing me off since September." He was getting more and more aggressive, scarring Lis's pot of gel eyeliner with hard jabs of his brush while they both worked from a makeup tutorial on Youtube. Lis reminded him it was only October. "It's like, the way she inserts herself into every little thing, like girl: just be okay with the fact that not everyone wants to be your friend. It's a lesson we *all* learn, and grow from it! And the way she fucking acts like Tyler's mother when he barely even talks to her anymore? It's hard to watch."

It was true. Lis was surprised that Tyler wasn't confiding much in Madison these days. She expected Madison to know that Lis was putting some distance between them, but either Tyler wasn't complaining, or he wasn't complaining to Madison. If it was the former, that worked for Lis, but if it was the latter, she felt sad for Madison. Just because she and Trevor didn't want to be her friend didn't mean she didn't deserve friends at all, and the heartbreak of a childhood friend giving you the cold shoulder was a plot ripped from of a Disney Channel movie Lis would be inappropriately moved by.

Lis reminded Trevor that he was due to graduate a year ahead of them, "One more semester, just breathe. Then she's mine and Silvia's problem."

"Don't say that, or I'll throw my scholarship to save myself the survivor's guilt."

Lis had been told very little about the Halloween show, except that she should be excited. Lis had been seen enough to be considered a regular at the bar, and had gotten to know a few of Ty's friends. She was now less Trevor's guest and more of an audience member in her own right, though she still arrived with Trevor every time. Max now seemed to be taking an interest in her, and she hoped that was a reflection of what Ty might be saying about her when she wasn't around. They kept up the daily texting and spending more and more time together after the shows were over. Trevor often asked her why she didn't just make a move, and she said that that would be cheating. She meant it, but not in the way Trevor thought she did. The way Lis meant it had nothing to do with Tyler; instead, what she meant was that she didn't want to take a shortcut. She didn't want to rush to the good parts with Ty, she wanted to watch things play out and see what might happen. And, if Ty made the first move, she couldn't be held accountable for what happened next.

The show started extra late, which she'd learned was a good sign, as it usually meant something spectacular was brewing. Max looked incredible, cinched within an inch of her life so that she cut the perfect black widow silhouette. She was Morticia Addams with a few latex touches that made her shine when she moved. Every performer she summoned brought fake blood with them. Or maybe real blood, it got blurry in a few spots. There was dancing, stripping, bondage, needles, and warnings so one could choose what they saw. It was all the magic of a regular show, but the sex and blood were turned up to eleven and smeared with Vaseline. Lis wished she could move like they did; maybe someday she'd learn. At intermission, the audience was breathless and warm, but since it was quite cold, only a few people took the opportunity for a smoke break. Lis and Ty stayed in the bar, waiting for Ty's people and Trevor—*their* friends, Lis realized, not just hers and his. While sipping from glasses slippery with condensation, Ty told her his plans for the night.

"So, it's getting colder out. Too cold to stay out late, I think."

This was terribly disappointing. Lis looked forward to their post-show winddowns at the bar, and if the weather meant those would be on hold until spring, she would be devastated.

"Are you leaving right after this?" She asked.

Ty turned the question around in his head. He was taking serious pauses, as if to clue her in to the fact that there was more to what he was trying to say than his words.

"Well, I thought I might leave that up to you. My apartment isn't far."

"You're inviting me over?"

"Yes."

Lis ticked her head in the direction of their friends, who were stubbing out their cigarettes on the way back in.

"Are they coming?"

Ty shook his head during another heavy pause, a light shake, and smiled.

"No."

...

Ty shared an apartment in Bushwick with Max and one other person whose name Lis never learned and whose face she never saw. Ty showed her into the entryway after a short walk from the bar. He gestured toward the not-Max roommate's bedroom just off the main hall. "He's from Jersey, you know him?" he joked. Lis didn't know if Ty talked about the roommate in terms of "him vs. us" because he was straight or because he worked in an office. The apartment was surprisingly nice, the catch was that it was on the fifth floor and there was no elevator. All the rooms were equal-sized, Ty's faced west. While passing Max's door, Lis saw piles of fabric, fuzz, some leashes scattered on the floor, open train cases of cosmetics with leaking tubes of gloss spilling out, and an overfilled ashtray. Seeing Max's mess endeared her to Lis, and though Lis wanted to keep looking and making out more artifacts of Max, Ty was leading her to a door in the back of the apartment, past the kitchen/living room. Lis saw the fire escape from which Ty had photographed the sunset for her. Traces of cigarette ash clung to the places where the sill met the wall, remnants of what she imagined were many wistful evenings he spent breathing smoke into the night air. Also on the windowsill was a lonely, bleached-out amethyst and what looked like a deer's jawbone. "The view makes it the best room, but the other two don't know the cardinal directions so they let me have it before they knew what they agreed to. They didn't want the hassle of having the emergency exit window." All walls except one were covered in posters and prints advertising movies and musicians she'd never heard of; the final wall was exposed brick, and it was blank only because Ty didn't know how to use a masonry bit. His bed, which had no headboard, was pushed up against it; a pillow at the back of a modest arrangement served the purpose of being stuck to the wall to keep heads from cracking open. When Lis was invited to sit on his bed, her movement caused the pillowcase to make little velcro noises as it was pushed and pulled on the bricks.

Lis wasn't sure what was going to happen at first. She knew what she wanted to happen, that this was the part where flirting became cheating, but did that mean that she was supposed to come on to him, or did she continue to wait for Ty's moves? She was nervous. The way things had gone with Tyler made her worry that she wasn't cut out for being a sexual person, not yet. Then, Ty kissed her. Lis had always thought smokers were supposed to taste bad, but that turned out to be a myth. He kissed her slowly, many times in a row, and not once did it occur to her to fear breaking his nose with her forehead or smacking her spit unattractively.

Ty used his hands. He carefully and subtly guided her so that before she knew it, she was laying down while he propped himself up sort of over her, sort of next to her. He didn't box her in with his forearms like Tyler did. As they kissed, she began to respond with her own hands, grabbing his hair, his face, his shoulders. She became both senseless and hypervigilant. When his hand made its way under her skirt, she pulsed like a nerve. This time, like she'd imagined, her shirt and skirt were still on. Her tights were pulled down to her knees, his shirt came off. She breathed heavy, and he didn't constantly look at her for reassurance. He asked her if she wanted to be fucked. When she said yes, he grabbed a harness, as if out of thin air. His thrusts were not like Tyler's. He was smooth, consistent, and his eyes on hers didn't embarrass her. Still, it didn't feel as good as she knew it could, so she touched herself, un-shy this time. Ty liked it, and offered to take over. She was afraid that if he did, she might not come, which seemed like a real possibility this time. Still, she let him. His touch was different than hers, but he timed his fingers with his hips, and stroked her until she came.

After, they spilled out onto his bed and talked.

"Can I ask about your tattoos?"

Ty leaned over the side of the bed to fish a cigarette out of the carton in his jeans pocket. Lis noticed that she was nearly fully clothed while he only had his boxers on. She thought about taking her shirt off, but it seemed awkward to do so after he'd already been inside of her. "Sure," he said.

Lis pointed to a date written on the soft skin under his bicep. "What's that?"

"Ah, shit. That's the first one, it's my T date."

"You don't like it?"

"I thought it was really original when I got it, but that was before I knew any other trans people."

It was hard for Lis to imagine him not existing among his own kind.

"In general, being trans feels really original when you only hang out with cis people."

"Sounds scary, to be alone in a group."

"It is, when you're lonely. Now I can feel embarrassed about it. Who hangs out with cis people anymore?"

He turned and smirked at her. It took a second, but she got it. "Who, me?"

He laughed, hard.

"Did you forget?"

"I guess so."

Lis was sleepy. She was comfortable enough to go to bed with Ty, and she wondered if she could make it work. Who would miss her? Who would look for her? How un-suspicious could she be about it? Sometimes she thought being a good actress meant being a good liar. Lis was not a dishonest person, but her ability to lie well did make her feel guilty, as if she wouldn't be able to make it telling the truth, as if the forces that guide evolution had given her the lying genes knowing that it was a talent she would need to survive. She thought again about Ty's boxers, and about how he didn't ask her to do anything for him. Despite the good time she'd had, she felt somewhat disappointed that he wouldn't fully undress in front of her, and not only because she wanted to see him naked. She felt like whatever impression she made on Ty hadn't convinced him that she was safe. She wondered if with someone else he might have taken his boxers off and asked for more. As she began to get up and prepare for an expensive ride home, he told her she could stay if she wanted to. She *did* want to, and she hoped desperately that he believed her and that it didn't sound like a lie when she told him she had to be back in the dorms. He walked her to his building's door, and kissed her one more time before she got in the car. "You'll be around next week, right?" He asked. "Of course," she said.

2017

The bar served great food. Few places they went to did, but Max had secured a guest spot at a show they'd never been to before. She was excited, because the venue was nicer than usual and she didn't have to be on stage all night. It was jarringly bright, which is to say they the soft glowing overhead lights were on, rather than the primary light source being a half-dead fluorescent bulb and scattered neon signs. It wasn't an especially ritzy bar, just a notch above what they were given to expect. Ty, Lita, Silvia, and Nat formed the pod of support for Max, and during intermission they took a spot at one of the bar's booths to rest and drink. Ty was being unusually lush. The pharmacy had still not gotten in touch with him to renew his prescription, so he was feeling unmoored. As such, he ordered more drinks, hoping that if he could stay sober after all of them, it'd be proof of some kind of inner stability.

Air conditioning pumped through the bar enough to make everyone comfortable, but there was no pretending it wasn't the dog days of summer. "Can we do a beach day soon?" Nat asked the group.

"Please. We still need to take you to Riis," said Silvia. "And you, too," she added, nodding at Lita, who hadn't been in New York long enough to have gone. "Sucks that your surgery date isn't until the 28th, you'll have to wait for your first topless beach day."

"I don't know, from what I've heard of Riis I might just say 'fuck it' and have a topless beach day this year."

"Nice," said Lita, squinting at him with an appreciation for his moxie that made Ty want to roll his eyes. If they even made it to Riis before the end of August, he doubted that Nat would put his money where his mouth was.

The first half of the show had been good, but none of them wanted to gush too much until Max had her chance to perform in the second. For the first time in a long time, Ty put some effort into his dress—well, as much as he could, given the heat. Oddly, Nat wasn't wearing something obnoxious. Perhaps it was being away from their home bar, or he'd simply run out of fruity binders. Though the shirt was still tight as a seventies roller skater's and the shorts had barely five inches on the inseam, it was conservative, for Nat. There was something about Nat's hips and the way they were so ramrod straight, making only the slightest of violin shapes out of his torso that made Ty look, fascinated, and he felt control over his eye muscles get away from him.

Lita got up, "How much time do we have left, five minutes at least? That's enough for a cigarette, right?" Silvia nodded, and the two of them eased out of the bar to have a quick smoke break, leaving just Ty and Nat in the booth. Nat waved them off, and then returned both of his hands to his drink, sitting the way a child would.

Ty shouldn't have had so much to drink, but his intoxication was not from the drinks alone. Nat was wearing some kind of perfume that smelled like peppercorns and oranges, and every time Ty leaned back to expunge the scent from his nose he could only smell the kitchens. He couldn't find any clear air to breathe. It was either the heavy garlic and oregano fumes coming out of the kitchen, or he was trapped by the sweet molecules drifting out from behind Nat's ears. He would have gotten up to go outside but he felt glued to his seat, and to escape he'd have to say "excuse me" more times than he felt able. If he were still a smoker, he would have had an excuse to wriggle away with Lita and Silvia and get some fresh air. What his brain fog protected him from was that he didn't want to get up at all. He was exactly where he wanted to be. If he could be completely honest with himself, he would know this was because he was alone with Nat, not in spite of it. When Nat's thigh touched his, and Ty regretted that he'd worn jeans instead of shorts. He wanted to touch him, and so he did, then he quickly snatched his hand back like he'd come to after being hypnotized by a cursed emerald.

Nat sat comfortably in the booth, but his eyes snapped side-ways to catch the movements of Ty's hand. Dazed, Ty saw him as though he were some kind of trickster god; a Hermes, or maybe a Loki, what with the Scandinavian thing Nat had going on in his family. Ty was horribly embarrassed, and Nat looked confused, but before either could speak, Lita was rushing back to the table with a half-burnt cigarette still in her mouth. Somehow, she'd heard the act two ushering music from outside before either of the boys in the booth did. "We did *not* have five minutes!" They hustled back to the stage. Ty realized he'd started something, because the heat coming off of Nat as they stood next to each other while watching the show was very different from your typical crowded-room-in-August heat. That perfume cooked on his skin, Ty wondered if anyone else was smelling it as strongly as he was. Ty was feeling something painfully confusing, but luckily the good mood of the bar and his drinking were sheltering him enough to feel okay. It wasn't attraction, or regret, it was the anguished gratitude of a hyper-conscious ego watching the id grab at things they wanted.

All Ty remembered of Max's number was that she wore crimson and that she looked beautiful. Immediately after bows, Nat and Ty called a car and sped off to their apartment.

It was better than it had been the last time. Nat, specifically, was better. When they got in the door, Ty was unsure how to pick up from where they'd left off at the bar, but he didn't have to think much; Nat brought their faces as close as they could be without touching. "You want this?" He asked. Ty could only nod. "I won't touch you until you make me believe it." Ty grabbed Nat by the back of his neck with enough force to shatter their teeth. Ty barely had to speak before there were hands on him, exactly where they needed to be. There were no straps or anything else besides tongues on bodies. They ended up in Nat's bedroom, where Ty felt that he might faint from the overwhelming sensation of coming into a mouth instead of his own hand, as he'd been doing for too long. "You're such a hypocrite" Nat said, briefly coming up for air. Ty meant to say "don't" or "stop" but he said both to achieve the opposite meaning. Nat dug his nails into Ty's legs while pulling him close; Ty tipped his hips into Nat's mouth, arcing his spine. When he was finished, he still had energy, and the fierce desire to reciprocate. Cliche images of dams breaking and icecaps melting played in his head, but what it really felt like was agency. Control, in the absence of his overactive mind. Nat's body was much different than the one Ty had fucked two years ago, but this was better. The differences, the fact that there was more between his legs for Ty to hold in his mouth held a special significance for Ty; it meant that there was a barrier between this night and the last night. It was also the first time he'd been so close to a body made the same way his was.

Ty was having an embodied out-of-body experience. He was fully in tune with himself—and with Nat—in a way he rarely was, but he could also see and feel his body from a distance. The image of himself between Nat's legs, Nat's fingers pulling his hair, was something he could see so perfectly, an exercise in perfect proprioception. As Nat came in his mouth, he felt like he did on the night of the open set when he'd made eye contact with himself in the bar's bathroom mirror. It was like he was wanting himself; the act of being desirable to someone else made him want to be in his body more than he ever had. It wouldn't be like this with anyone else though, and in that moment he was suited to accept that fact for as long as he could stay conscious before falling asleep on Nat's stomach.

8

2015

Erik and Lis spoke on the phone very few weeks. Erik was 5 years younger than Lis—his impending birth had ended their parents separation and near-divorce back in 2000. After Erik, and 9/11, Lis's parents forged a bond under the Patriot Act. They made it through 2008 blaming the misfortunes of some of their neighbors on their inability to be a "real American family," though in that period they did have vicious fights over her dad's insistence that her mom stay at work instead of transitioning to stay-at-home motherhood like she'd been planning to.

Lis used to beat the shit out of Erik when they were little. She often had to explain this to Tyler, an only child, who didn't understand that sibling fights are bloodsport. Especially when one combatant is twice the size of the other but still too young to know her own strength. When Lis got into high school, Erik was easier to be around. He was smart for his age, and funny, and they found a few things in common. They began to play video games together, taking turns, one watching the other play and providing color commentary. This first semester at the dorms had been an exercise in learning how to be the daughter in another state. It improved all her family relationships; with Erik because she missed him, and with her parents because she wasn't in close quarters with them.

Erik was talking through the crumbs in his mouth. "So, I hope you're bringing Ty's full FBI profile to Thanksgiving."

Lis had never called Tyler "Ty", but Erik decided on the affectation to be funny, so she let him. Now though, with the emergence of a real Ty, it was jarring. Erik's question was a warning in light disguise. "Oh fuck, why?" She asked. While listening to Erik, she was pulling clothes out of a dryer in the dorms laundry room. The machines were free, but they didn't lock, so out of paranoia, Lis had spent the last hour watching her things tumble around.

"Dude, mom asks me about him *constantly*. She thinks I know his address and what his parents are like, she swears there's shit you're not telling her, and she keeps telling me 'you have to watch out for your sister.'"

"You're thirteen."

"I know! What the fuck am I gonna do? Besides, it's not like you even tell me anything." This was true, as Lis had few facts of value about Tyler. Lis could hear a bag crinkle on the other line as Erik grabbed more to eat. "But she keeps saying it and I think she's trying to say that I'm supposed to keep you from getting date raped or something." She heard him brush his fingers off on his pants or bedspread and return to clacking buttons on a DualShock controller.

"From Jersey?"

"Yeah. She says whenever she asks you about him you talk like you barely know him, but I just told her that four months wasn't that long? Then she told me it was different for girls."

"Four months? And FYI, it's not different for girls." She felt it to be her responsibility to try to correct the things her parents taught Erik.

"Yeah, August, September, October, and this is November, right?"

"Oh, yeah." Her brother knew the age of her relationship better than she did.

"Uh, anyway, now that you'll be here in the flesh next week she's going to harass you about it."

"Can't she do that on the phone?"

"I guess she wants me and dad to be witnesses."

"Does dad say anything?"

"Like ever? No. He doesn't even speak up to change the subject. When he opens his mouth it's like watching a heart monitor go off."

Lis's mother, Frances, had been anxious about Lis's love life for years, and her dad, Robert, was not typically a quiet guy, so to know that he was now apparently shut tight at the subject was a cause for concern. He always had equal measure of criticism and encouragement to give, but it always sounded facetious, like he read a book on parenting for men and all he could do now was recite from it. She appreciated the warning from Erik, but it didn't do much good. She intended to go home for Thanksgiving without bringing any more knowledge of Tyler than what she already had. This way, all her answers could be honest, which would make her mother's frustration all the more satisfying. Lis didn't hate her mother, but her mother could be irritating in ways that were not simply annoying, but tragic. She knew her mother was okay with the things Lis wanted to do with her life, but her mother also wanted to have a nice daughter, and eventually a married daughter, and Lis's lack of interest in her boyfriend made her anxious for her character and her future prospects. Frances could accept some unorthodoxy, but not too much. When Lis was in middle school and *Glee* and *Degrassi* were airing episodes about queer teens, her mother thought it was very nice that Lis was so tolerant, and told her that she was special and perfect and that she was so glad to have such a nice daughter. The way Frances affirmed her gratitude for Lis every time the subject came up was suspicious, as if she were insinuating that Lis's nice daughterhood were the best trait she could have, the one she should protect with her life. This was confirmed when Lis was fifteen and her mother explained to her that she had to be careful with her virginity and that if she couldn't give it to her husband, she'd better give it to someone nice. *Did you give yours to Dad?*, Lis asked. *No, I didn't, but I gave it to a sweet boyfriend and let me tell you, it was a* very *nice experience.* At that, Lis ended the conversation.

Lis's mother was cloned in the extended family, which was two-thirds aunts. There were some fun aunts, others were less pleasant, and Aunt Theresa was downright venomous. They'd all be present for Thanksgiving at Lis's mother's house, since Lis's mother was the oldest and most established and the one who made the arrangements for her grandparents assisted living. Lis's parents didn't have the nicest home—that would belong to Aunt Theresa—but their home was big enough to fit a good number of people in a cozy way that was only slightly claustrophobic.

The one thing that made Lis grateful for Port Authority was that unlike most of her classmates, who had to roll giant bags around school all day and leave in the middle of class to call cabs for JFK, she only needed to catch a bus. At the other end of the line in Jersey, Erik and her mother were waiting for her with the Volvo, a silver one that made her very feel very elite in middle school. Lis got a tight squeeze from her mother once she entered her orbit. Her mother's hugs were brief, but tight. Lis noticed that her mother was wearing an unusual amount of perfume, which she only did for special occasions. Lis quickly realized that *she* was the special occasion.

"Oh my god, everyone's so excited to hear from you, big exciting girl from New York!" While she talked, Frances's fingers nearly flew off the steering wheel, her nails springing up and folding back in like the spines of a bluffing reptile. Her charm bracelet rattled.

"Who's everyone?" Lis asked

"You know, everyone! The aunts, the cousins, the *little people.*"

Lis tried to exchange a look with Erik, but he was trying to get through a tricky level of *Angry Birds.* "Ah, *that* everyone."

"And you know my work friends want to hear about it too, but they have to settle for hearing it secondhand from me. Maybe I can get them to come over before you leave. You know, Annette asks about you all the time because her cousin went to your school back when it was Catholic! She's a nurse now. It used to be a very popular school for nurses."

Lis had heard this many times. There was still an abbey in a townhouse near the school, sometimes she'd see the sisters pushing laundry in carts in their habits. Presumably the hamper bags were full of wimples. "Oh wow."

"Yep, she said last she heard, it still looked like a girls' school to her, because, *you know.* Isn't that funny?" Lis wasn't sure if her mother expected that she would laugh at the casual homophobia.

"It's where I met Tyler." She countered.

"Oh sure, it's just a joke sweetheart." Frances rolled her eyes.

Erik tuned in to say, "Maybe I'll go there mom."

Frances shook her head like it was a joke and her hair dusted off her shoulders like car wash pillars. "Oh honey, come on." She shook her head again, tossing her bangs around. She kept a pair of glasses on the dashboard now.

"Anyway, we got a big dinner tomorrow, I'll start cooking at noon and you can help. Remember how you loved to help me when you were little? I thought maybe now you've been away for a while so you'd like to again. And Aunt Peggy is coming early, so she's going to help too, we'll have a little girls' time, we'll catch up, and then people start coming around two, and then we eat at four, sound good?" Frances's plans were never set in stone. By tomorrow, Aunt Peggy would show up earlier than she said she would, she'd probably bring one of her kids instead of letting them come later with their dad, two people would come on time and the rest would come in a bum rush at three, and Frances would get distracted by a hundred different things so they wouldn't eat until six. Lis agreed with her anyway. Her phone buzzed with a text from Ty. Erik noticed. "Ooh, a message from your lover."

Lis turned bright red, and her palms began to sweat before she realized that Erik was just teasing her about a message that he thought was coming from her boyfriend. To spite him, she reached over and poked his phone screen at random, disturbing the manuever he was trying to use to get a high score. "Aah what the fuck!". Lis opened the message. *Would you think it was corny if i missed you?* Her chest fluttered, and she looked out the window at the scenery on the way back to her parents' home.

2017

The sun rose early; it was only a few minutes past four am when Ty opened his eyes, wondering how long he'd been out and barely feeling Nat's arm over his stomach. He remembered everything, including how much he'd enjoyed himself. On waking, it felt like his life was being shoved back into his skull without lube. He looked out the window in Nat's bedroom, at the dark pink sky. He couldn't actually see the sun, just the rays it was starting to cast on the clouds that surrounded the building. This morning, the fourth floor felt like a high rise. The brain in his head felt coated in caramel, sticky and glossy. He waited for the consequences of his own actions, which came quickly. He had a few minutes of feeling like his life was easy; as the blue started to appear in the window he remembered himself, and began to edge out of the sheets gently, so as not to wake Nat. Getting the arm off his chest was the tricky part; he grabbed a pillow off the floor and made a switch. He did not look at Nat as he left the room, picking his clothes up off the floor. Maybe Nat wasn't completely asleep when he shut the door behind him—it didn't matter, he was out safely, and free to go back to his room for more sleep. He was wired, but he wanted to be unconscious.

Ty was so unsteady getting into bed that he clacked his head against the brick wall his bed was pushed up against. For a moment, thinking about Nat's warm and soft body under the covers and his own clammy body outside of them, he was disappointed to be back in his right mind. In his own bed, which was cold and dry from having been empty all night, Ty felt the night fall out of his ears. Consequences, consequences. This would be bad.

When he woke up again, he could tell Max was home. Her first meal of the day was always coffee and chili-lime cucumbers. Her stomach was strong. Ty wanted to sit with his friend and have coffee with her, but he realized that he was scared to go out there and have his new secret blown up, as Nat was sure to be unsubtle and touchy. This would not stay a secret for long. Ty gave in to some moments of self-loathing, knowing that if he was now uneasy in his own home it was his fault. *Fuck it,* he thought. He put on a shirt and made for the coffee urn. Max looked unmoved and unbothered, sitting on the couch with a red-streaked empty bowl in her lap. "Hey," she said with her croaking morning voice. "Yeah," said Ty. Nat was awake but still in his room, ever a late-riser. Ty nipped at some coffee, feeling it drip into his empty stomach. He could tell that if he pulled up his shirt he'd see the curve of his skin dip concave between his hips—a nice feeling he tried not to treasure too much. He got out bread and butter for toast, something to soak up everything he'd had at the bar. His mouth, shockingly, did not feel rotten. Did he brush his teeth before? Possibly. His memory was skipping in the wrong places.

Nat came out. He and Max and Ty exchanged more exhausted monosyllabic morning greetings. Nat did not so much as look at Ty while pouring himself his own coffee and returning to his room. Odd—or good? Ty tried to remember what every morning was like, and if Nat was being frosty or normal. Max didn't seem to notice anything strange. What time had she gotten home? Was it before or after Nat's room got quiet? Ty hoped she hadn't heard anything. More specifically, he hoped she didn't hear *him*, not really caring if she thought Nat brought someone else home last night. For a moment, he wished that he'd brought Nat into his room so that Max might think Ty's dry spell was over without realizing who with.

Ty's stomach crunched against his will, almost knocking him over. As long as he could remember, this had never happened to him before. It felt too dramatic to grab at his stomach or groan, so instead he squeezed his brows together and closed his eyes while freezing in place. "You alright?" Max asked. Ty breathed for a moment before answering, "Mm-hmm, stomach isn't right." Max shook her head, "Eat some toast love, you have a hangover. No wonder, you were half a river deep last night."

"You saw that?"

"You didn't embarrass yourself, you just overdid it. Lita let me know that Nat put you in an Uber and got you back here. You probably owe him a twenty for the ride."

"Mm."

This was not a hangover, but he went to the bathroom anyway and found the problem easily. A greasy smear of red pooled in the dead center of his underwear, rippling crookedly across the seam of his briefs. The underwear he used to wear had cotton panels in the crotch especially for this kind of thing, but the ones he wore now weren't built for it. It had never been a problem, T had taken care of both bleeding and discharge, but his last shot had been six weeks ago. He would go to the pharmacy today and be a cunt if he had to, maybe if he could get his prescription filled he'd be able to do his shot and the bleeding would stop. The last time this happened was nearly four years ago, and Ty wondered how bad for him it was to be now shedding the accumulated tissue from those years. He'd never had cramps like this before, no wonder he didn't recognize them.

If he got on the phone with the pharmacy now, he'd be able to avoid Nat for at least forty-five minutes, so he called. It was a Sunday and the phone lines were slammed. It took twenty-seven minutes to be connected with a pharmacist, a person whose voice he'd never heard before. It was always a new voice. "Hi, I haven't gotten a new prescription and it's been weeks," he said. "Date of birth?" Ty gave them a date from the winter of 1992. There was the sound of typing on the other end, and he was asked to confirm his name and address, only to be told "I don't see a prescription here from your provider, it might be too early for you to request a new prescription since this is a controlled substance."

"I know, but my vial ran out six weeks ago."

"Oh, okay yeah I see that you were allowed to request a new one in May."

"Right, and I did."

"Um.... okay, so what I'll do is send a message to your provider to ask for a new prescription."

"I'm pretty sure that's been done already."

"I can mark the message as urgent if you want."

"Yes, please do."

"Here, I'll send them a message, and I'll transfer you to the front desk line so you can leave a voicemail for her, okay? They'll probably get it done faster if you ask too."

"Alright, sure."

The pharmacist transferred him, and the phone rang for fifteen minutes before the line dropped. In that time, he heard Nat get up, wash his face, and leave for work. Ty had to figure out what to do about the bleeding, since no one in the apartment kept pads or tampons around. He was housebound until he could get some lest he risk walking to Duane Reade with a stain on his pants, and Max had a show that night. He texted Silvia, *can i ask you to do me a favor?* She got back to him after thirty minutes, *Sorry, I was teaching a class, whats wrong?*

i need tampons

Shit. ok I'll come over.

thanks.

What absorbency?

regular and maybe a backup box of super. and pads to be safe i guess. ill venmo you

Dont worry about it.

Silvia could always be counted on to be an angel.

9

Being in her parents' home meant Lis couldn't stay in her room longer than thirty minutes without feeling guilty. Before college, she spent most of her time in here, slouching in her bed or on the carpet with her computer. She was nostalgic for that cloistered privacy, since now she had so little of it. In her dorm bunk at night, she was surrounded by the bedtime lumps of Madison or Silvia asleep in their beds. She was looking forward to nighttime, after everyone was fed and asleep and she could be alone. As she went down the stairs, she realized she'd forgotten what it felt like to walk on so much wall-to-wall carpeting—it was like getting her sea legs. The first floor was starting to heat up with humid warmth from the oven. So far, smells from the kitchen included burnt residue and grease while the double oven pre-heated, white wine, and ice, but in a few hours it would all smell like the store bought Italian seasoning mix that mummified Frances's cooking. Lis dreaded finding out what kind of help she was expected to provide, and hoped it wasn't anything to do with gutting the bird. Luckily, Aunt Peggy was already there, packing the innards into a gallon-sized ziploc. When Lis entered, Peggy was already mid-sentence. "I'm writing the date on these Franny, you gotta use them quick even in the freezer, otherwise they lose all the good stuff. And here she is! Look at *you*, come here. Oh my god, you're still getting taller! But that's okay, I kept growing until I was in my mid-twenties, and Brian doesn't mind a tall girl—lots of boys don't mind a tall girl. You get it from Grandma Helen, all the Norwegians are like that you know, they get tall and big to chop down the Christmas trees—"

Frances was already tired of her sister and shoved a big bottle into her hands to cut her off. "Peg, could you put this in a bowl or something? I want the champagne to look nice."

"Oh sure, honey. Gotta make it look nice now that Lizzie can drink with us, we gotta impress her."

Two glasses of Pinot Grigio were on the granite top, one half full and the other nearly drained. Lis noticed which lipstick marks corresponded to which woman and found an explanation for why Aunt Peggy was so chatty. Her mother steered her to a cutting board with four bleach-white onions and asked her if she knew how to chop them, then proceeded to demonstrate without waiting for an answer. Lis worked on this for as long as she could, both to kill time and to impress her mother with the final product. She rubbed the papery skins off the cutting board and drew the chopping knife down in slow firm strokes, using the knuckles of her left hand as a guide to get thin little slices that could melt in a pan. After fifteen minutes, she presented the onions to her mother. "Oh, those are gonna burn." Frances took the onions away, and tried to make the best of it. "It's fine, it'll be fine. We have to put more oil on it and we have to wait to put them in, that's it. Just... next time, do it how I showed you. But this will be fine."

Lis was not given another task.

By then a few more relatives had shown up, her Aunts Ida and Donna, Donna's husband, and both Ida and Donna's kids. The cousins from Ida were older than Lis, children of her first marriage that began and ended before Lis was born. Donna had one son a year younger than Erik and a toddler who was still cute and blessedly quiet. Lis had never been very close with any of them, but her older cousins were nice enough. Tommy was working in electric now, and Jessica hadn't decided yet, but their grandmother was encouraging her to go to beauty school like she had. This was tall Grandma Helen, who'd supported her family on a hairdresser's wage, supplemented by Grandpa Tom's income from the sanitation department. Grandma Helen was in her mid-eighties now; she and Grandpa Tom had limited mobility, so they'd be catching an access-a-ride provided by their assisted living facility to Thanksgiving.

Every person who came through the unlocked front door worked their way past Erik and Lis's dad to come say hi to "the girls." Every aunt who passed through got stuck here, joining the cooking or drinking wine and moving plates around. Jessica escaped by staying close to Tommy and making small talk with Erik. Lis was stunned by how her entire family, whether related by blood or by marriage, looked the same. They were a hive of pale beige people with green or blue eyes, all moving and hovering around each other with eerily similar mannerisms. Coming home was an exercise in thawing out. These were people she'd known her entire life, and yet it took a few hours to get used to them again after a separation. She found herself circling her mother or falling in with whichever aunt was her current favorite.

Lis watched how her mother talked to Jessica, asking her how school was going, if she would give her a hair and makeup discount at the next family function, if she had a steady boyfriend, and she wondered if that was who she'd become if Erik ever had daughters. When she talked to her aunts, she wondered if their interest in nieces came from a need to tour the paths their own lives could have taken, and if they did the same with their daughters. Lis knew that her mother was proud of her for getting into a four-year school in the city, and that she was tickled by the thought of her daughter one day becoming a rich and famous actress,—even if she complained about the cost of tuition for a "dreamer degree"—but Lis also knew that her mother would have liked Lis to stay close to home, to go to Ramapo or somewhere where she could come home on the weekends—the city wasn't even too far for Lis to do that now, but she and her mother both knew that that was more to keep her occupied in the city on weekends than there would be up at Ramapo.

The house got uncomfortably warm as the cooking went on, but nobody wanted to open a window because of the chill. Lis wanted to step outside onto the screened-in patio, but that was where Aunt Donna and Tommy took smoke breaks, and she didn't want to talk to either of them. Despite Lis's lack of romantic activity until now, around the time she turned thirteen Donna had gotten the idea that Lis was some kind of hussy. Every time they saw each other, Donna advised her to put a sweater on, to stay away from boys, to make sure she got home at a good hour every night, and asked her where she kept the guardian angel charm Grandma Helen gave all the girls when they were little. Lis kept it in the drawstring velvet bag it came in in a box in her closet, but that was not an answer to give Donna, who expected all the girls to keep it on her person at all times. Donna was the last of her sisters to have kids, so maybe something about watching Jessica and Lis grow up made her anxious. Or maybe Donna was just annoying and felt superior to everyone else because she went to church more than they did and had crosses and angel paintings all over her ugly popcorn ceiling house to prove it. No matter the reason, Lis tried to stay away from her. As for Tommy, she suspected that he was a libertarian and stayed away.

After a few hours, the house was full. The access-a-ride came late, and was the source of much complaining, but ultimately Grandma Helen and Grandpa Tom were deposited safely at Lis's family home. When she went to greet them, Helen patted Lis's face like she was a mound of dough. Tom took Lis's hand, kissed it, and said "prettier every year." The dinner itself wasn't bad, Lis sat in a strategic formation between Erik and her father. Lis's father was a quiet man, and none of these people were related to him. His family was much smaller and older than Frances's; both of his brothers relocated to Florida a few years ago, and his parents were long dead. He had a decent rapport with Uncle Tim, which meant Lis only had to contend with Erik, Aunt Marie, and Aunt Peggy, which was perfectly survivable. Since Peggy had already had her shot at Lis during the dinner prep, she focused her attentions on Erik, who played the easily-loved scamp that all the aunts loved to pinch. Being near her brother made these gatherings much more bearable for Lis.

By ten, the party was nearly over, but Lis didn't return to her room until the last of the stragglers (Peggy) had left and her mother had thrice made it clear that she was "ex*hausted,*" finally punctuating this by putting her wine glass in the dishwasher. She hugged Lis and said goodnight, and they parted ways at the bottom of the stairs. Lis went up, hearing Erik's X-Box pinging. He only got away with playing this late because their parents slept downstairs on the other side of the house. When Lis entered her room, she realized with several shivers that she hadn't closed the window before dinner. Though she was chilled, the cold air made her feel better. When she was overwhelmed, it felt like her brain was swelling and needed to be iced. The chill approximated that. She stripped off her family clothes and curled up under the covers, letting the window stay open as it had been for the past twelve hours. Her mother would complain about the waste of a heating bill. This room that she'd spent most of her life in felt so strange now, as if the ceilings were three feet taller than they'd once been, and laying in her bed felt like being at the bottom of a drained pool. She knew she wouldn't sleep until well past midnight, so she put her headphones in and reviewed her YouTube subscriptions, eventually opting to revisit old videos, trying to pinpoint the average period at which one who is on injectable testosterone begins to pass. Five months, perhaps?

At around two in the morning, she got a text. She slid open her phone screen, ignoring the "Happy Thanksgiving" messages from Tyler and her roommates she'd received hours ago. The new message was from Ty, and read: *you up?* When she answered yes, he sent her a photo. It was another image from his fire escape window, showing off the big yellow full moon. The moon she could see in New Jersey was crowded by stars. Beautiful stars, but show-stealing ones. She preferred Ty's moon, the one that shone independently against the night sky, the only light strong enough to be seen amidst the city's light pollution. She asked him why he was awake, and he briefly told her that some worries were keeping him up. *Talking to you helps*, he said, *you want to come by when you get back?* Of course she did. Thinking about Ty, about the ways he touched her and looked at her, she felt perfectly warm in the chilled expanse of her childhood bedroom. The next morning, she'd be subject to various criticisms of her sluggishness, but that night, she felt no shame in staying up into the wee hours to send messages back and forth with Ty.

2017

Being the only person he knew with an office job, Ty was often alone in the apartment on weekends. Nat usually had to work a shift at the cafe, and Max was out walking a dog, or dashing to doors, or one of another variety of gig jobs to sustain herself alongside her drag income. It was good of Silvia to come over and keep him distracted for a bit. At least, that's what he thought would happen, but it was clear from the moment Silvia walked in the door with tampons and pads and a few treats that the night before had not been very discreet. She had a smile on her face, not a big bright one, but a slim one that skewed to the side of her face, an "oh, you're in trouble" smile. They sat on the couch and put episodes of *Drag Race* for background noise;

neither of them watched it anymore, but there were usually one or two people per season that they'd seen or knew, and that made it compelling. Now that Ty was properly bleeding, he knew the cramps he'd been having were a mechanism for wringing him out. He hoped that maybe the pain and its intensity were indications that his system was trying to get through this as soon as possible. His periods in adolescence had been two weeks long, and he was dearly hoping that wouldn't be the case for him this time.

Silvia picked apart the wrapper of a Hershey's kiss, and before she put it in her mouth she said, "So, you and Nat left early last night." It wasn't a question, it was a sentence that requested completion. It was like she was playing call-and-response with him. He liked Silvia a lot, and didn't see how he could lie. "Yep." She nodded like a therapist, and then said, "You know, sometimes orgasm triggers spotting."

"You've got to be kidding me."

"Yeah, it's a little frightening, but normal. The pharmacy's been fucking you over, right?"

"Six weeks since my last shot."

"Fuck, that sucks. Sorry."

Ty shook his head. "It's not the worst thing that's happened to me this week." At this, Silvia looked at him with her head cocked, like he was doing a bad job of lying to her. "You want to tell me about the worst thing that's happened to you this week, then?" Ty liked Silvia so much that sometimes he forgot that she was Nat's close friend, and perhaps not amenable to his being openly repulsed by being associated with him in a sexual capacity. "Worst might be an exaggeration," he said. She softened. "I liked seeing you two having fun together. It's been a while."

"Mm. Two years."

"Two years is a decent amount of time, Ty. I thought you were past this?"

"Of course I am."

"Right, right. That's why you let him come live with you. And hang around you all the time. And then you go home together. You're totally past it and ready for a fresh start." She clapped a little bit to tease him.

"What happened yesterday was a lapse in judgement. If it hadn't been Nat it would have been someone else."

"Who?"

"I don't know, someone."

"After a two year sex drought you have one extra drink and then you can go pick up anyone?"

"Aren't I in enough pain?"

"I'm just saying, that doesn't sound like you, even if you'd been plastered. You don't just sleep with *anyone*, you have to think about them for at least three weeks first, you've always been like that."

Silvia was right. Ty remembered the time he'd slept with her, how it had come several weeks after she started going to the bars, and how he'd run the idea of asking her out by several friends to confirm that it was a reasonable thing to do. Nothing ever came of it except for one good night, but their friendship had bloomed out of it so beautifully that he could not regret that she was not his other half. He did not take the matter of who he might go home with lightly. In the long period of celibacy that began and ended with Nat, this was something he'd forgotten about himself. He tried to think about what happened last night and how upset he really was over it. He came up against a dense wall, not like bricks, but more like a thorny hedge. If he really wanted to he could get through it, but painfully. In his current cramped-up state he did not feel equipped to take on any more discomfort.

Ty thought that maybe he could guess at something that would make it all make sense: the satisfaction from Saturday night and the reluctance of Sunday. He tried, "I just don't want to live like a teenager anymore, and being with him makes me feel like I'll never grow up," but when Silvia asked if he really believed that, he gave up, knowing that Nat's immaturity may be annoying, but it wasn't insurmountable. He thought harder, in the imaginative space of his brain rather than the one that contained the hedged-in truth. In the time he spent thinking, Silvia watched, as if looking for signs of meltdown. "Ty, are you bothered about the timing of Nat's coming out?"

"What do you mean?"

"It happened so soon after you two called it off. I know it's irrational, but it wouldn't be unusual for you to read something into that, when you're hurt."

"Nat did what he had to do, like everyone else does. The timing is what it is."

"So you're fine with it."

"Didn't you say it wouldn't be unusual to be hurt?"

"So you *were* hurt?"

"Fuck, *am*. I *am* hurt. It's irrational and shitty, but what am I supposed to feel? I feel like I was toured. Like I was a test run. And I can't be mad at him because then what? I know he's not making it up—no one does—it's real and that almost makes it worse."

Silvia let out a sigh. She turned down the volume on the television to dilute the noise of people having panic attacks while thrashing around to Donna Summer. "I think you made it feel safe for him. You know, he saw what it would really be like to live the way that he wanted to, and you caught him at a bad time in his life. I think maybe if you met him after all that you'd feel differently about him, but given the way things turned out I don't know if he would be *him* without you."

"That's a lot of fucking pressure."

"I know," she put a hand on his leg, "but it's just the way it is. I don't know if it's fair to expect anything different." Ty leaned into her, and she put her arm around him. It reminded him of his adolescence, the way girls used to hold him at sleepovers while they watched movies together. He sighed through another cramp.

"Why is it so easy for him?"

"I think that when that dam opened for him, he let it keep going. He gave himself permission for *everything*."

"Yeah, I transitioned too, why am I like this?"

Silvia held him just a little bit tighter, her way of softening what she needed to say. "You think too much and not enough at the same time... and you are very cruel to yourself."

It got to be early evening, when the sky got bright, bright red and Max and Nat were due home in a few hours. Silvia had to be on her way to Lita's. She could have offered to bring Ty over, but she didn't want to. Not because she didn't want him over, but because she knew that if she gave him a reason to be out when Nat got home, he'd jump for it. When Silvia left, Ty felt scared. Not of her, but of the fact that he was not a good secret-keeper. This thing with Nat was already spinning out to the point where friends had expectations of him that he didn't want to be held to. Like any good friend, he wanted Silvia and Lita to be happy with him, but when it came to this, he couldn't just give them what they wanted because they thought it was a good idea. He had to believe it was a good idea himself.

Silvia left her smell behind on the couch. It comforted Ty, and made him hope that maybe he could weave something out of his hardwired head that would make everyone happy, including himself. He was stressed and ill, and couldn't shake the feeling that he was sitting in a pool of his own blood, causing him to compulsively run to the bathroom to check and fear sitting on anything upholstered for too long. It was getting late. He worried about Max in the summer. In the winter, she spent the extra money it took to split cabs home with friends, but in summers she just walked or took the train. He could tell that his emotions were out of key. As if he didn't already know his self-control was slippery, further confirmation came in the boiling stomach and quickened pulse that came with anxiety. He forgot what this felt like. When he was healthy, in good humor, his fears lived in his chest and his brain; his reflexes were sharper. If something moved suddenly or was about to fall, he caught it. Before, he might not have noticed if a projectile flew right past his face—he'd gotten socked in the collarbone by a stray softball that way. In his current state, he did not feel ready for anything.

IO

2015

Since Lis had returned home from Thanksgiving, it had been much easier to make plans with Tyler. Their scene presentation was the next big event of the semester, and the last before auditions. This meant that making or accepting time with Tyler was only to agree to a rehearsal, and that she could easily feign exhaustion if he wanted to do anything afterward without him being able to say she hadn't just spent upwards of an hour with him. Lis and Tyler worked their scrap of *Who's Afraid of Virgina Woolf?* until the words were incoherent and Lis mumbled them in her sleep. Whenever they workshopped it in class, their professor gave them the same critique: the scene needed more heat. Lis and Tyler were instructed to be unafraid of making the audience uncomfortable, to treat them like the kids in a messy divorce. It was good advice that Lis took seriously; she practiced being messier. She watched clips from the film adaptation over and over, Liz Taylor zipped into an uncomfortable-looking dress, shrieking at her maybe-gay husband. She looked like she smelled like perfume over oxidized foundation and cold chicken out of the fridge at midnight. Lis knew what that felt like, minus the heavy drinking. She tapped into how she felt getting back to the dorms from Brooklyn, now that she was there nearly every weekend. Sometimes Lis wondered why Tyler never asked where she was on Saturdays, but she assumed he had something to do that was keeping him occupied.

Lis was able to get to Brooklyn much more now that Silvia was in the thick of winter showcase rehearsals. Trevor brought her out every weekend, sometimes more often, and she was experimenting with new bars, meeting new people, and everywhere she went, there was Ty. It began to feel more like she was cheating on Ty than she was on Tyler. Between nights out and rehearsals she was burning out, but on the bright side, she was sleeping better. She spent fewer and fewer nights up late with her YouTube subscriptions. Life was blowing up like a balloon animal; meeting its limit in some places and only beginning to take shape in others. When she'd graduated high school, the contours of her future were just about solid, but now she felt like there were new things to anticipate, and she was having trouble identifying her place in the rest of her life. She was even questioning the work she did; did she actually want to be in movies? Was it possible that other stages awaited her, or other ways to be a character? It was much too late to change her major now.

Lis was confident in her own performance, whether Tyler sunk or swam did not concern her as much as it should. Ever since they'd slept together, she felt like whatever she might have owed him as a girlfriend was satisfied. He hadn't tried to invite her back again, but when they were together, even in public, his kisses were too warm, and his hands on her were too slippery. She was thinking of breaking up with him, but they saw each other tolerably little, so she thought she could juggle him along with everything else she had to deal with. He was low maintenance. Even so, she was fairly certain that they'd be broken up over the winter break. She didn't want the next semester to begin before she could be free of him—and free to pursue Ty in the open.

On the day of final presentations, they were called up third. Lis and Tyler had come up with their own simple blocking; they were to enter the classroom door, stumbling over each other and the threshold; Lis would clamber to the "fridge" they'd made out of two stacked rehearsal cubes while Tyler sat at the tiny bistro table that portrayed the dining set. Lis would wobble around the space, sitting on anything but a chair, while Tyler was supposed to sit miserably at the dining table. The scene got off to a bad start when Tyler decided to throw his arm around Lis as they walked through the door, behaving like a sloppy frat boy who needed help getting home. His arm was heavy, hot, and limp, and its weight made her shorter and irritated from the top. It only got worse. Lis did her best to pull of a sophisticated drunkenness, as if she were fifty years old with a wealth of pith, but it was hard to bring that out when her show-husband was being an asshole. Something had gotten into Tyler. Instead of playing the meek husband with a barely-concealed violent streak, he was doing his best John Belushi.

As they went on, Tyler let an edge sink into his voice. For a moment, Lis hoped that he was dropping the goofy "I'm just as drunk as you" bit and committing to the character as they'd agreed on. In the ten minutes they had to perform, Lis felt a true repulsion, as in, she could not remember why or if she'd ever felt attracted to Tyler. She hoped that maybe that would work to her advantage. When he was supposed to approach her for the big finale, he got much closer than he should have and stroked her face, like a villain who had her strapped to a chair. He chose to freeze there, waiting for the professor to acknowledge that the scene was over. She stared at Tyler, closer than she'd been in a long time, hating him. Their classmates were completely silent.

The professor cleared his throat and said, "Alright, thank you for that." He turned around in his chair like he was backing out of a parking lot to look at the other students. "So there was a lot to see there, yes?" Lis looked at her classmates, seeing on their faces expressions ranging from entertained to deeply disturbed. It seemed that some of them thought she and Tyler did a fine job, which frightened Lis, because these were the same students whose every scene was delivered like it was pulled from back episodes of *Glee*. Their taste was not to be trusted.

Their professor turned back to them. "I don't think I can fault you for taking my direction, but I should have been more specific. Tyler, you're coming in a little too hot, Lis, it seems like you're ready to flay him alive, which is not altogether a bad thing, but it's all here," he gestured above his head, "with no levels. Right now what I'm seeing looks like he's attacking you, but this scene.... We have a marriage, yes? A relationship gone cold, they hate each other's guts. They're actually on the same page in a lot of respects, but they haven't figured out how to leave. Right now you two don't seem to be on the same page. Lis, it looks like you *do* know how to leave, but Tyler wants you to stay. So lets try it again, yes?"

And then they had to do it again. And then once more. Each

time Tyler clung to some shred of inappropriately horny energy, while Lis tried her best to cool him down. It was clear from the tone of the room that nobody was satisfied with how they left off, but the professor eventually let them stop. Lis wondered how responsible she'd be held for Tyler's performance. They sat back down in their seats next to each other to watch the next few scenes. One of their classmates decided to bring real jell-o as a prop to throw at his scene partner while they also acted out a messy divorcing couple's fight. They got applause at the end of theirs, and only had to do it one more time. While one of them scraped jell-o off the wall to set the next go around, Tyler had the nerve to try to hold Lis's hand. His face looked deceptively innocent, as if nothing bad had happened to him just now, nor ever. She pulled her hand away, not jerkily, but firmly enough to make it clear that she didn't want him to touch her.

Lis was fucking miserable. The thought of having to work with Tyler again was enough to make her want to quit her major. She felt betrayed, as if Tyler had deliberately sabotaged their scene. None of the other runs they'd done in class had been this bad, in fact, some had been pretty good. It horrified her to think that Tyler felt at liberty to fuck with their scene so suddenly. This was her work. She was especially concerned to think that he was entitled enough to grope her in front of their classmates. His affection disgusted her, and it wasn't necessarily his fault. She felt somewhat guilty that her instincts were coming up against him so hard, but when he was near her she couldn't help it. All she wanted was to get away from him. To stay with him was unsustainable. She turned on a switch in her brain to get her cells used to breaking up with him and being single again.

It was an uncomfortable, scary train of thought, but she hoped that if she started planning for it now she'd be able to make it happen before winter break and feel decent about it. After all, she thought with some self-satisfaction, it was unlikely that she'd be single for very long.

2017

The door to the apartment had such a loud bolt that you could hear it from any room no matter how many doors were closed. The neighbor's dogs would bark when they heard it un-latch, so that no one could sneak in or out of any of the units on their floor. Ty heard the barking, the clinking, and the prolonged key negotiation that signaled Nat's return. As the newest room-mate, he still hadn't quite gotten the handle of the maneuvers needed to get inside. He entered in his work clothes, stained with coffee and sugar, smelling like bleach from cleaning the store at closing. Ty remembered well how the bleach would soak into his hands and make them smell fishy until he got home and scrubbed them with steel wool. When there wasn't steel wool, sometimes he'd come up with an excuse to handle an onion, just to get the scent off quicker. Ty had not yet moved from the couch; he was sprawled out, exhausted, fresh from a run to the bathroom to check that tampons did indeed still function as he remembered them.

On seeing him this way, Nat asked, "You alright?"

"Yeah, I'm okay."

"Okay." He set his bag down, and turned into the first door off the entryway, his bedroom. He shook out his hair, releasing the smell of coffee, and started to strip. Ty did not look. Nat came out in just his pajama shorts and binder, and approached Ty with his hands half-up, an expression of decision on his face. "So, are you planning to ghost me? Or something?"

"What? We live together."

"Uh-huh. Well, I woke up alone this morning, and you don't want to look me in the eye right now. This is a very different vibe than the one I got when we were fucking last night."

Ty flushed. The eight-hour shift had clearly given Nat time to think, and the thinking made him angry. He turned to look at him, hoping that eye contact would calm him down a bit and by proving him wrong on at least one count this would be easier, but Nat did not seem very impressed. Ty tried to remember what Silvia said to him, but this felt like being thrown into a rose bush, and the effort of pulling himself out did not help him find grace to put into his words.

"I'm not ghosting you, and I'm not trying to act like nothing happened. I just, don't think I was thinking rationally and I regret giving you the wrong impression."

For a moment, Nat froze. Ty wondered if it was too reckless to hope.

"Do you remember saying 'please'? You said it like six times with your dick in my mouth."

"Jesus Christ."

"I'll bet you regret it, but that doesn't mean you didn't want it."

"I was drink—"

"Oh fuck that. *You* put your hands on *me*. It was *your* idea to 'leave early,' remember?"

"Keep your voice down."

"*Nobody* is here!"

A silence passed that made the air seem more tender than it was.

"Just when I thought some progress had been made. Stupid fucking me, I guess. Why don't you just say you're embarrassed to be seen leaving a club with me? That you're embarrassed to have fucked me, and you're terrified that people are gonna find out?"

Ty glared pointedly. "First time being a mistake, huh?"

"Oh my *god*. You were not this much of a pity party when I met you, what the fuck happened?"

"What the fuck happened? What do you *mean* what the fuck happened?"

"*Me?* No no no no, *this* is not how we revisit this. Do you not remember me texting the shit out of you? Practically begging to talk to you so I could apologize? If you'd given me the chance you would have gotten a sorry way bigger than what was necessary. I don't know what I could have done to make you feel more wanted. '*Mistake.*' Please spare me."

"What exactly would you have apologized for?"

"I don't know, for having a boyfriend that I didn't even like that much? For lying?"

"It would have been a pretty piss-poor apology then."

For a few moments, it was difficult to tell if a turning point had been reached. Had they hit something? A breakthrough? Was this the progress Nat wanted? Or did they still have more arguing to do? Nat's face clenched, hissing breath from his nostrils. Ty wanted to see a scavenger dog licking his chops, but instead he saw a bruising in Nat's eyes that was difficult to look at. There was some real pain there, and ashamed as he was to think it, Ty knew that he could not touch that yet. It was easier to pretend that Nat felt no pain at all. Nat's eyes narrowed. "Are you getting so worked up because I'm the only person who's fucked you in the last two years?"

This made it easier for Ty to suspend his disbelief in the fullness of Nat's emotions. He'd never seen Nat hold his own in an argument before, and wondered where he learned it from.

"No, Nat. I'm 'worked up' because you used me for fucking character development."

Nat's head snapped back and his brows creased in a gesture of incredulity.

"*How* does that make any sense?"

He didn't want to say it, because there was no way to do it without implying that he thought Nat was a kind of copycat, one whose choices lacked sincerity and who instead siphoned traits from the people around him. As he faltered and failed to answer, it was clear that Nat was turning it over in his head, that this was truly the first time it had occurred to him that anything other than his old boyfriend was stuck in Ty's craw. His eyes melted a bit, giving Ty a better view of the hurt he'd seen in there earlier, and his mouth twisted like he was shaken by what he started to realize.

"Don't you know it's not about you?"

This was a question Ty had thought in the direction of various people in his life. His mother, his brother, his first lesbian friends at school. The people who thought that the way he turned out was due to some unconscious influence on their part. It wasn't incorrect for them to think that their relationships to him shaped him, but it was incorrect for them to assume they had the power to create a person. He felt breathless. He felt things stuck in him, scraps of fabric on torn branches that he needed to retrieve, one-by-one, so that he could put them together and make something. Again, he tried to think about spending last night with Nat, how preferable that was to fighting with Nat, and he was dismayed to find himself coming up against that same hedge. What he'd said wasn't a lie, but it wasn't the whole truth. Seeing how sad Nat looked, Ty wished he knew what the truth was so that they could share it. In the meantime, he tried to explain himself.

"That's the whole point. It *wasn't* about me. All that time we spent together was about *you*. It was a backdrop for *you*, a learning curve for *you*. Nothing was starting, you were never going to be serious about me, you just needed to see that it wasn't so scary on the other side after all, and to figure that out, you picked me."

Nat and Ty looked at each other, weary. The quieter it got, the more the air in the room depressurized, the more Ty thought about Max and how she should be home soon. He wanted to see her, to tell her about this and see if maybe she could help him. He wanted someone to pick at his brain and loosen what needed to be loosened in order for him to understand himself. As he heard the sounds of Max's boots coming up the stairs, the dogs next door picking up the sound and filling their lungs to announce her, Nat began to retreat to his door. He gave Ty one last look as Max's key turned in the lock.

"You're wrong."

II

2015

After the scene presentation, Lis made plans to go to Ty's again, if he'd have her. Going away for Thanksgiving and the slog of rehearsal and Trevor-supervised nights out had kept her from going to his apartment again, despite desperately wanting to. She had made a loose plan to end things with Tyler when school ended for winter break. When they first got together, she thought that the best course for their relationship would be to remain together until the conclusion of senior year when graduation and career needs pulled them apart, but she couldn't keep up the pretense anymore. Winter break was just three weeks away, and in the meantime she had work to do. Finals were coming, and auditions for the spring play, which she was doomed to bomb; her scene presentation had shattered any confidence that had happened to accumulate over the semester. She just needed to get through the next three weeks, avoid him, and then have a hard conversation before school broke until January. Breaking up before Christmas was not according to plan, but she never thought Tyler could repulse her so much, and she never could have planned for Ty. She knew that once it was over, she'd feel terrible. Not for herself, but for Tyler. He was only horrifying her because he was her boyfriend. Once he became some guy, just another actor in her major, someone who didn't feel compelled to touch her, she'd pity him.

Now that she knew things with Tyler were doomed, she became more fixated on Ty. She didn't want to think about having to return to Jersey for the break and being separated from him, and from everyone else. She was looking forward to January, when things with Tyler would be over and she didn't have to lie anymore; she'd been sloppy with this secret, and was only getting sloppier. There was only a little bit of fear. Of Ty, of what being single and fucking Ty meant, as opposed to having a boyfriend and fucking Ty. But they'd only fucked once, so to find out, she'd have to keep doing it. And there was a good chance that Ty didn't want anything more with her. But all through the Thanksgiving trip, and the time she spent futilely working on her scene, he'd been texting her. Ever since they exchanged numbers, they'd been having one continuous conversation. She knew that there was something else going on. Would they be dating when she got back to New York after winter break? Was she sure that was what she wanted?

There was a show that weekend, but she wanted to see Ty sooner, in the daylight, so she sent him a text.

hey, what are you up to the rest of this week?

He replied quickly. *you got time to come down to brooklyn?* She loved that he seemed to know what she was thinking.

i need to get away from the dorms for at least a few hours tomorrow? I work until 2, but you can come meet me and we can do whatever you want

I love that, but you have to figure out something for us to do. I dont know where anything is in brooklyn.

Ty had mentioned his job a few times, a cafe near Prospect Park. He said it was more stressful than working with coffee should be, by virtue of the high-maintenance clientele that populated the area. When she got there, he was breathless, clocking out in as much of a rush as he could muster.

She flagged him down after he'd tossed his apron and emerged from behind the counter, "You that eager to see me?" she asked. He responded, "I'd love to flatter you, but I'm always this eager to leave."

He took her to the bookstore two doors down from his job. It was a tiny store, but one where a good hour could be killed. They wandered around looking at the shelves of used books—there was only one rack of fresh printings. Though the store was small, it gave the impression that every book one could ever want was within it. Lis looked for the queer section, and found a one foot cubby with a few memoirs and photography collections. She pondered the slim pickings, which drew Ty over. He said that it was a decent selection in the tone of someone who rarely expects more than a blank space. Lis understood this. Thanks to her Youtube habits, she'd listened to the unanimous complaint from FTMs that no one ever talked about them. Lis wanted to see for herself if perhaps they just weren't looking hard enough. When she did her googles, she didn't find a complete absence of FTM representation, but what she found was rarely appealing. There was a decent handful of memoir and real-life experience books that one could find in bookstores like the one she was currently in, but when it came to fiction, or television, or movies, it was like trans men were a rumor that no one was much interested in. In general, a trans person could gain good ratings, but only if they were sufficiently miserable. The few trans men on screen seemed to either be very sad lesbians, or assholes, and were consistently played by "daring" cis actresses in limp flannel outfits and bad hats.

Lis considered buying something from the queer section, but she was too worried about choosing the wrong thing in front of Ty, so they left. They considered going out, but the early December chill was not worth the wander, so instead they took the train back to Ty's and ordered in. This time, they were not alone in the apartment. Max was home, making preparations and final touches to her look for the following night. By now, Lis and Max knew each other, but not as well as Lis knew some of Ty's other friends, since Max was always busy giving shows. At first, Lis thought that Max never turned off her stage persona, but she soon realized that the stage persona was not a character. Before Trevor ever took her out, she only saw drag queens at a distance or through a screen. In the life she lived now, her real life, she was seeing queens up close. The reality of knowing them was entirely different animal than the figure of the drag queen she studied on television. Queens like Max were both more subdued and more vibrant, in the sense that they were more human, as humans are when they fully exercise their capacity to create.

Lis and Ty ate in Ty's living room. Lis expected to end up in his bedroom, but to her surprise and comfort, they had what felt like a simple little date. Even if Max was in and out of the room and they weren't necessarily alone, it felt intimate. Perhaps not more intimate than the last time Lis was here, but warmer. Not an alternative, but a growth. A new stage of whatever was happening between them. She liked it, and thought that if this was what it would be like to be Ty's partner, maybe there was nothing to be afraid of. She thought about sleeping over, but the commute from Brooklyn to campus was too long to attempt in the morning, and besides, Trevor was around, having gone out for drinks with someone he met at the bar a few weeks ago, and he promised to meet her so they could make the evening train ride home together. Trevor knew that Lis felt safer with him at night. Trevor was tall, his dancer's body more than capable of defense, or at least he looked buff enough that she didn't worry much about being threatened when she was with him. During the day she got many across-the-street and down the block shouts from men whose words were flirtatious but whose bodies looked ready to box her in if she got too close to a wall. At this time of year it was already dark out when she left her late PM classes, and sandy-headed men in beige pants and baby blue H&M button-ups bulged out of the stinking brown-paneled faux-Irish pubs to offer her coke and tell her to pull her coat tighter when she walked by. There were fewer men like that in Ty's neighborhood, and they were more likely to be wearing athleisure and floppy haircuts, but they were just a different flavor of a figure she would never be rid of.

Trevor picked her up from Ty's apartment close to nine; she couldn't believe she'd been there for so long any more than she could believe the little kiss Ty put on her cheek as she left. So chaste. She and Trevor walked down the Ty's street, to the trains.

There was nothing outwardly unusual about her or Trevor, so when the disembodied voice screamed "faggots" at them and her ears filled with vinegar, she wondered what they'd done wrong, and which one of them he was talking to. They hurried down the lit subway entrance quickly, relieved to know they weren't being followed. Whoever the shouter was, he was apparently an opportunist rather than a predator. Even so, Lis's hands shook while refilling her Metrocard, ashamed of herself to see that Trevor's hands were so steady that he swiped his card correctly on the first try and helped her when she had three swipes come back null. She wanted him to say something, something funny and light and sharp that she would never think of. She at least wanted him to say something about his own date, but the entire forty-five minute ride home sounded only like the thrumming noise of the express line along the tracks. At one point, the tracks screeched horribly, and it sounded like there was a nest of vipers hissing and spitting under their feet.

2017

Nat never wore button-ups, so into his duffel bag he packed some rolled-up zipper hoodies and a single blouse that he'd gotten for cheap at H&M. Ty had offered to loan some shirts of his a few weeks ago, a gesture of terse goodwill that was forgotten now that they weren't speaking. Since their fight, they had been avoiding each other as best they could in their apartment, assisted by work schedules. Nat had been picking up more night shifts lately.

Months ago, though he would never say so out loud, Ty

expected that he and Nat might have had a few days of friendship preceding his surgery, especially in light of the fact that Nat was about to be isolated in New Jersey for two weeks while he allowed his mother to watch over him. Ty didn't know exactly what those friendship days might look like; maybe instead of icing him out, Ty would be nice, offer more than just a few shirts, like advice, or the pillow he had used to learn how to sleep on his back. Maybe they'd do things together like go get lunch, or go to a museum. Things that they might have done years ago and never got around to. Maybe they would text. What Ty was anticipating was something like a renewal, a dam-bursting that could perhaps demolish his reticence and restore a relationship. The current circumstance was a perverted inverse of what he'd been thinking of; he'd gone too far, gotten too excited, and he now faced the consequences of his own bad behavior.

Max had no need to avoid Nat. Sometimes, when he could hear that the two of them were in the living room at the same time, Ty kept his ear out in case they said anything about him. Of course they never did, knowing that the doors were hardly soundproof. It was a self-centered thing to think.

It was raining, a yellow-y thunderstorm drizzle that seemed likely to turn into a hard storm. The cars outside made paper tearing sounds as they skidded down the street. Ty thought about going into the city. He had no reason to, except maybe to press the pharmacy and see if they had his prescription, but he liked the way that the rain fell and cleaned the streets. Manhattan looked its best when the lights shone on wet streets. Brooklyn in the rain turned red and green, and it was beautiful too, but the lights weren't the same. He grabbed his wallet and keys and threw them in the side pocket of a backpack, thought about bringing a book for the train and decided against it, knowing it would get soaked. Unluckily, he and Nat opened their doors at the same time, each bound for the same station, same direction. Nat was in work clothes, a mild outfit for the bus to New Jersey. He looked tired.

"Good luck." Ty meant it.

"Thank you."

Nat had already said his goodbyes to Max and Silvia and Lita the night before. Ty felt sorry for him, for the fact that he wouldn't be seeing his friends for the next two weeks, that nobody was coming with him. Nat pulled his bag around him, grabbed an umbrella, and left; Ty felt guilty for being the last person he saw before going, it seemed like the kind of thing to leave a bad taste in both their mouths. After the door closed, the apartment felt quieter than it ever had, and Ty stood in his doorway for a few minutes, waiting until he could be sure that Nat had gotten far enough ahead to be on the train to Port Authority already, wondering if he should even leave the house. Sitting inside all day, even with the excuse of the rainstorm, would make him feel depressed. It would still be light out for a few hours, late summer's daylight holding out well into September. At first, he opened up a few windows to let the smell of the thunderstorm in. He thought that maybe that would be enough to make him feel like he'd been outside without the effort, but his restless leg kicked in and he had to stay up. He realized that Nat had taken his umbrella, so he put on a hoodie and vowed to brave it.

The thunder cracked a few times before any drops started to fall, Ty only got a little wet before ducking into the train and taking it up to Herald Square, a central location where he could either make it a point to run errands or just wander. The rain was the same temperature as his body and offered no relief from the heat, so the air conditioned car felt incredible on his damp clothes. He was sure his hair would look hideous after this outing. It was starting to get shaggy and chin length, almost like Nat's. He would have to make an appointment with his barber to get his sides re-shaved soon, or ask Max to help him. Once he was off the train, the rain had picked up so much that he was instantly soaked through. Even so, he was not angry with Nat for taking his umbrella. He started to walk west, in the vague direction of his pharmacy, though quite a bit further uptown. Herald Square was still crowded, a sign that the rain must have heaved just a few minutes before disembarking—his luck. Rains like this made all the grey concrete steps up to townhouses and the sidewalks warm, like there were traces of amber or honey in the stone. People often complained about the stink when it rained, but he couldn't smell it. It was one of those things, like not knowing the difference between types of trees or how to work a garbage disposal, that came with growing up here.

He soundtracked his walk with a band whose singer had just been revealed to be an abuser a few weeks ago. Prior to those revelations, Ty loved the band, listening to their music non-stop, even planning to attend an album-signing a few days before the news broke. Now, he managed to suppress the earworms and brain itches for their melodies until times like this, when he was entirely alone and feeling sure enough that no one would know. Once he finished, he cleared his phone of any proof that he'd done this.

It was hard not to think about Nat. Ty wondered if surgery might change him, if he'd be a different kind of person when he got back. Then again, Ty could have been imagining that New Jersey was just a place where Nat went to transform and come back, as had been the case for as long as they'd known each other. He heard Nat on the phone sometimes with his mother, a woman who Ty only knew as a voice that alternately shouted and gave dead monotone answers on speakerphone beyond Nat's door. Nat seemed to think that his door was made of stone with the way he made noise behind it. With his mother, Nat discussed things like his job, and his lack of good acting gigs, Nat explained that it was hard to find a gig that would take him, though it rather seemed to Ty that Nat just didn't audition, and his mother complained about the money wasted on a degree that she and her husband hadn't wanted him to get in the first place. Nat asked what he was supposed to do instead, STEM? She talked about applying oneself and business majors, and didn't Nat have that roommate with a good job? And then Nat would say that Ty was different without explaining why, and his mother didn't ask either, she just kept pushing about how Nat should consider going back to school, she'd pay for it, under the condition he studied something worthy. Ty would sit and wonder what Nat meant when he said he was different.

Nat and his mother *never* talked about his transition. Even now that he was going back there to recover from surgery in an odd arrangement that had him going there only to be driven back into the city and out again after an overnight stay, his mother only called it his "procedure." Ty imagined that Nat would be stuck upstairs in his bedroom while his family spent their time downstairs in the rooms filled with his old pictures and talking about their lives and the directions they'd gone in since Nat officially left home and moved into the apartment. There was a brother who was going to school now, majoring in economics somewhere local, and though Ty had no real clue, he thought he could safely assume this was the favored child. Nat talked about his brother with affection though, so it couldn't be that bad.

Ty hoped that the surgery would calm Nat down. In a way, he almost hoped it would disappoint him. Not like a botching, but in the sense that he wanted Nat to understand it wasn't that big a deal after all. In Ty's own experience, the excitement faded in a few weeks and he had to come back to the same old life he'd always had. Maybe if Nat mellowed out, Ty would be able to work with that. He tried to imagine having a boyfriend, which was moderately easy, and then he tried to imagine that boyfriend being Nat, which made him nearly keel over in the street. Thinking about a romantic entanglement with Nat was akin to a disorder of the inner ear. In this state, he could hardly imagine how easy it had been to sleep with Nat. It had been nearly a month, and now Nat would be gone for a while, and Ty was too absorbed in his neuroses to realize that he would miss him.

If he didn't know Nat, things might be easier. Nat made a very good first impression by being attractive, funny, and intelligent without being a snob. However, Ty did know Nat. Subconsciously, Ty thought he might know things about Nat that Nat didn't know himself. What Ty had the most trouble with was that Nat post-transition had adopted a quality of adolescence that most trans men did when they came out. This was something often painted with broadly romantic strokes, a kind of reclamatory Peter Pan syndrome that symbolized the capture of a lost boyhood; to Ty, it was no different than a man-child's refusal to grow up. It seemed to Ty that every trans guy he knew was a late bloomer. None of them could arrive on time to anything: haircuts, button shirts, conclusions. It frustrated him, more so because he knew he'd had his own adult teenhood phase and was no better than Nat in this respect. Even now, he still had blushing nights in bed wondering if he'd ever rid himself of that completely. To think that at the age of twenty five he might still have the stunted clumsy brain of a teenager horrified him, and he closely examined himself routinely to try to sweep it away.

12

2015

The semester was at that stage when people who thought a lot about their resumes crunched. Lis hadn't studied much since high school, when she fruitlessly scanned pages of formulas in a half-hearted but sincerely stressed effort to see if maybe she could score above a 70 on at least one math test. At this point, she'd finished both of the required math courses (designed to be passable for future actors), so while her peers dealt with their blood pressure, all she really had to worry about was the tedium of writing a few papers. Instead of worrying about those, she let herself withdraw into her anger over the way her scene work with Tyler had gone. Her anger was real, but more importantly, it relieved her from social obligations. She didn't have to go see him as she could distance herself on the pretense of being offended, and all her school friends were clogging their schedules with test prep and practice for audition week. Rather than put any energy into her audition monologue, she spent her days almost entirely in bed. She streamed a few shows and movies, but what made her feel like she was running despite sitting was a video binge triggered by a vlogger she'd never seen before. It was always exciting when this happened; a familiar story got a new look, and she set high expectations for what new information she might get from this new character's journey. When the story ended up following the usual framework, she wasn't necessarily disappointed, but there was a faint fatigue. Then again, it wasn't really any of her business to be upset.

This wasn't to say that nothing new ever happened in the YouTube forum of trans men, but when it did, when a new subject cropped up about a new way to resist gender roles, or dress, or wear makeup, or new myths about healthcare to quash, it seemed like everyone made a video about it in the same week and said just about the same thing, with minor differences in the language they used to affirm the viewer that whatever they were doing was valid. She knew there were some bad actors in the mix, people whose visions were limited and whose voices were more keen to instruct than educate, but she never touched those videos because she didn't have the energy to piss herself off.

This new vlogger was interesting. He was handsome in a more effete way than usual. He was an American living in Norway, which made her think he must be smooth sailing, but she was shocked to find that he still had trouble getting health care and clerical support, exacerbated by his ex-pat status. He also reported much of the same trouble in social settings that others did with having people get his pronouns right, though it was nice to be in a country that had never heard of and couldn't pronounce his old name. He talked about the bars he went to and never mentioned any other trans people, so Lis wondered if he was lonely. It was likely that he'd started making videos to attract a community to him that he couldn't find where he was. He mentioned a girlfriend in a few videos, but at some point in May of 2012 his descriptions of her started to veer in a direction so different that if this was the same woman, she must have gone through some kind of dramatic change. The pre-2012 girlfriend was athletic and distant, but rolled with his body easily. The one after was an affectionate asthmatic and always available, but seemed to be afraid of seeing him naked. One of his videos was about his thoughts on bottom surgery. The tone of these kinds of videos was interesting to Lis, because it sounded like almost none of them wanted it and those who did couldn't get it, but all of them loved to talk about it. This didn't stop the squeamish from wrinkling their noses when thinking about some of the more difficult aspects of metoidioplasty and phalloplasty—lots of people had trouble with the skin grafts—and these people were chastised in the comments section, usually by other channels, in which they were reminded that there are lots of guys who have these procedures done and it's not very kind or affirming to express disgust. Lis wanted to know where these guys were, because it would be refreshing to hear from someone who could actually speak with some kind of expertise. And yet, when she heard from one of her other go-to vloggers that there was a Photobucket-like site where one could look at nothing but bottom surgery results, she got too nervous to create an account.

In this new vlogger's video, he described the difficulties of trying to plan a procedure in a country where his grasp on the language was not the same as a native, and the unfortunate likelihood that if he were ever able to get the money, he would need to return to the U.S. for it. He described his family as supportive, but always in a hesitant tone of voice that made it clear to Lis that the support had limits. While watching him, Lis thought the things she usually did while hearing these men out. How does one get the nerve to change so completely? Did everyone have that capacity? She thought of herself, her life, and wondered if she'd ever feel so compelled to redirect the path she was on. Even if she blew things up, she would still feel so little, compared to all the things in the world there were to feel. She would never have room for it all. The vlogger upheld the custom of describing and defining the procedures in existence, and when she tuned this out, having heard it all before, she realized that at some point Madison had come home without her noticing and opened the door to stick her head in. Madison's expression indicated that she'd been paying attention for the last thirty seconds.

"Ew," she said.

"Madison!"

"Well not 'ew' *him*! Just like, 'ew ouch,' you know? Like 'ew please don't do that to me.'" She came closer, uninvited, and peeped at Lis's laptop. "He's cute. I was wondering what you were watching in here, is this for your social difference class?" Lis gave her stock excuse: *NoitjustcameupinmyrecommendedfeedandIgotcurious.* The social difference class was probably a better excuse, but the force of habit compelled her. Whatever she said seemed to be enough for Madison, who gave a brief "hmm," and left the room. It seemed that all she'd wanted was to spy on Lis. Restless, Lis pulled her blanket up around her face, and shoved some earbuds deep into her ears. Without expecting to, she fell asleep, bringing the videos into a dream with her. Lis's dreams were difficult, and didn't happen very often. She was usually so exhausted by the time she fell asleep that her brain had no energy to hallucinate, but she'd barely spent any energy all day, so in her nap dream every color was so vivid it screamed. She could see herself in this dream, not in the way of having an out-of-body experience, but in the way of being a different body that was not her own, and using this new body to approach the figure that she knew as her real body. When her dream-self's hands went out to touch her other body, she saw the tattoos and realized that she was Ty.

Every other want Lis had ever had was clear. They were things she'd decided on: a boyfriend, an outfit, long hair, to be pretty, to go to a good school. They were things she could understand, and maybe she was starting to understand something new, but the something was unprecedented, off-track. Nothing else she wanted or had wanted would work if she allowed the new un-nameable thing in. Without realizing it, she'd come to cherish being legible. It was a beauty to feel seen, to walk around the world with easy little words you could throw around, that others could catch in their hands, sticking to clothes like snow or dust, even if what they were seeing was false. She'd toured the world of illegibility, of being someone who didn't explain themselves. She loved those inexplicable people. Trevor, Silvia, Ty. Did she love Ty? Of course, but that love, too, was something that didn't explain itself. Was it illegible because it was for him or from him? After winter break, would she run straight into his arms, or would she turn tail? Did people love everything they missed? Could she survive missing what she had now, if it were gone?

Want, growing want, was threatening to sublimate her. In her dream, she knew that when it did, she would only regret wasting so much time building her future on an illusion. When she woke, though, she put that knowledge away, and moved to sit at her desk painting her nails, so that she'd be unable to use her hands for however long it took the varnish to dry.

2017

Ty tried to offer his mother home repairs. She lived in a three-bedroom ground floor apartment in Sunset Park that was renovated in the late eighties. The appliances functioned better than he did and were about his age. Though it was a rental, she was able to treat the place like she owned it by virtue of having a long-standing relationship with the landlord. As such, she never called the super for maintenance, but neither did she waste time on making repairs herself. Instead, she chose to clean over the cracks. The caulk was always rotting from the inside, though any smell it could generate was completely obliterated by the bleach powder she pasted into the seams every Sunday. Ty hadn't lived at home since he was twenty, and until then he simply accepted the pasted-over dishevelment of his mother's place. Now that he lived elsewhere he was hyper-aware of it, and hated the feeling that things were that way because she had no time and no one had a minute to spare for her. Ty had one older brother who'd moved to Staten Island with his girlfriend to live with her family after she got pregnant, and now had three kids, a job in electric that took him all over the boroughs, and no time to spend a weekend in Sunset tightening hinges. So Ty tried, but his mother turned him down. It hurt.

Ty's coming out seemed to be excruciating for his mother, who would call him in the morning and instead of saying anything, sob. He didn't know what he was supposed to say to her, since she wouldn't give him anything to work with, so she would cry, and he'd stay on the line with her until he couldn't take it anymore and told her he had to go to work. That stopped after a few months, and then they never spoke about it again. He saw her once a month, if that, and she wouldn't comment on his changing body. She reacted to his tattoos, but not his voice or beard. She called him by his new name, but sometimes she'd stutter, starting with the old one and bumping up against "Ty," flapping her hand like she was trying to get rid of a fly—but only when there was someone else in the room. Like he was a secret she was trying to keep. Ty's brother was a man whose shoulders gave you the impression he'd be large all the way down, but his feet were unusually small and thus he resembled a tooth. He didn't like Ty's business, but his vitriol was saved for trans women, who he thought were pedophiles coming after his kids. Ty often wondered if he knew that there were dangers enough within the family, and that if he was worried about his kids he should watch their relatives more closely. When he and Ty were together at holidays, he didn't say anything to antagonize, but he also didn't ask his daughters to hug uncle Ty the way he demanded that they give everyone else in the family kisses. Ty's nieces were sweet, and they liked him, but Ty knew that the best he could hope for was that they had good heads on their shoulders and didn't listen to their parents. He did not want to know what they thought he was.

Ty didn't go to his mother's that often, but he felt that he went often enough to prove that he cared about being a member of her family. Even so, the visits were tense and short. Ty had nothing to do there, and his mother had nothing to say to him. They'd never been very close, but Ty was his mother's only daughter, and her disappointment was so heavy it was practically a third child that lurked in corners whenever they were together. The disappointment was born in middle school, when it was already clear that Ty was not meant for the things she wanted him to be. His first girlfriend was a poorly kept secret his mother could barely stomach, a freckled soccer player named Shannon. Shannon now tended a bar at a chain restaurant; she hadn't spoken to Ty since high school, and if asked about him, she would call him "it." Shannon had been a terror, but she was someone who, back in the eighth grade, made him feel like a hint of his future self. She was mean, but funny, and her insults couldn't hurt that bad when they made him laugh at his own stupid self. They did not last through the summer, and though they'd never had sex, she started a rumor that he was so bad at going down on her he should give up on girls and go back to being straight. The results of such a rumor were that everyone thought Ty was a slut, but they couldn't decide how to pick on him, so they didn't. Still, when he was around, people didn't like to get to close to him. It was like, under his clothes, there was a stench that nobody could quite smell but everyone knew was there, as if their little primordial cavemen brains were being subconsciously alerted to the presence of an undesirable who wasn't quite a threat but certainly not a friend.

His mother kept a set of keys in a fake rock on her stoop, but Ty knew better than to use these, since one of them was rusted and warped by seasons and didn't fit into the second lock anymore. Instead, he rang the doorbell, and listened for her footsteps coming to answer the door. She worked for years on her feet as a nurse, and her joints were stiff; she was young yet and didn't have any trouble getting to a stand, but her huff of breath as she did so was audible through the door. She pulled open the hollow metal front door, and he held aside the caged screen to get in. They nodded at each other but did not say hello.

Coming here was something he did to prove that he was doing his part. If things were tense between him and his family, he did not want to give them the satisfaction of blaming it on him. For a long time, he insisted he was no different from them until he realized he wanted to be, and then when he stopped wasting his breath, nothing changed anyway. His mother looked exactly like him, even down to the over-processed hair and yellow nicotine nails. Since the last time Ty had quit smoking, his nails were not yet grown out enough to be clean. He cut them down to the quick every few weeks and ended up with persistent hangnails. His mother sat back on her couch and gestured to the kitchen with her left hand, "Manicott' in the kitchen, I made." Ty wasn't hungry, but he didn't want to refuse food. There was nothing out on the counter or the table, but there had to be food some-where, and he picked through a few shelves in the fridge until he found a dish of it covered in foil. He heated it in the microwave, taking a few silent moments in the wood-paneled and yellow-wallpapered kitchen. Ty's great-grandmother was German, and her husband was either Syrian or Greek, but all traces of that man were long gone after a violent divorce that occurred when Ty's grandmother was just a baby. The rest of his mother's gene pool was a hodge podge of miscellaneous middle European and English. Ty's father had been the same, but only a few traces of him remained after a quiet split that happened when Ty was five. His parents had never married. His brother saw their dad at his house upstate fairly often, Ty didn't. Anyway, Ty's mother only knew how to cook red-sauce Italian food. She kept zitis in the freezer through his whole childhood, making two every weekend and stashing them so that she could reliably skip cooking whenever she needed to during the week. Ty was certain that the reason his teeth were stained was because of all the tomato puree he'd eaten in various pastas and casseroles growing up.

When the microwave beeped, he pulled out the steaming pasta and broke it up to get the cold center to temper the molten sauce on the edges of the bowl. A childhood habit. He realized that his mother wouldn't want him to eat on her couch, so he sat at her table. He spent the first twenty-four minutes of his visit by himself in her kitchen, and then joined her in the living room. She put her book down and pulled her glasses down her nose to look at him and ask, "How's work?" He said, "Good, simple." She said, "Good," and put her glasses back up. This kind of dryness was predictable, as they had few things to talk about. There was nothing in his personal life that she'd want to know about, and he knew that her days were the same as they'd ever been: busy, tiring, and blue. If Ty didn't know that she had plenty of joyful days when he wasn't around he would feel bad for her, but he knew that on the weekends she visited with his nieces, that on free evenings when she wasn't too tired she went out with friends she'd kept since high school for dinner and drinks. They each had lives full of enrichment beyond each other, lives they didn't discuss. This is something that could have made Ty sad, but he was instead grateful. Grateful, because this kind of quiet, unobtrusive visit—if boring—was a hard-earned milestone.

He sat with her at her television as he always did when he was there, putting in the hours. When the sun set and it was clear that she had other things to do—on that night, it was pack for her weekend on Staten Island with her granddaughters— he gathered his things and left. On the train ride home, he experienced two track fires and signal maintenance, which he suspected was cover for another track fire.

13

2015

After her post-nap manicure, Lis emerged from the bedroom to find Silvia smoking a joint by the window. A surprise, since the night was still young and Trevor wasn't around. It wasn't often that Lis got to be alone with Silvia, and she wasn't sure she wanted to be now, since she looked very much the picture of having been in bed all day doing nothing productive and Silvia seemed to be enjoying some solitude of her own. When Silvia realized she wasn't alone, she gently turned her head over her shoulder and smiled, "Oh, hi love." The smile was like a glittering little gift. Silvia had done a three quarter turn from the window, inviting Lis in to stay or go if she wanted to. After a day alone, it was nice to have someone's interest, especially Silvia's.

"Hey. Trevor not around?" She replied, taking a seat beside Silvia. They sat close on the couch, leaning their chests against its back in order to put their faces to the cold chill at the half-open window.

"No, he wanted to find a hookup tonight and I didn't wanted to cramp him. What about you, nothing goin' on?"

"No, not really."

"It's nice sometimes, isn't it? To ignore the curriculum for a little bit and not feel scheduled?"

"Yeah... I think too much when it's quiet though."

"*Mm*, I get that. You want some of this?" Silvia held the joint out. Lis did want to try, but she felt embarrassed asking Silvia to show her how to smoke. She wished she'd let someone less impressive show her in high school.

"I'm good, but thanks."

"Of course. You alright? You sound... a little depressed."

"Yeah, I don't know. I'm a little worn out. I think the semester's dragging."

Silvia blew a stream of smoke through her teeth, aiming it at the bright windows of the building across the street. She was not the type of person to complain much, but Silvia would sometimes stare at this building and remark on how irritating it was for its residents to keep their curtains open so wide as if they were proud to show off in front of the whole city, because of course they *were* that proud. Silvia drew back a bit and said, gently, "I heard your scene presentation was rough."

"How'd you hear about that?"

"Madison said Tyler was asking her if you were mad at him."

"She didn't tell me that."

"Well, apparently she told him to ask you himself instead of hiding behind her."

"Oh shit."

"Right?"

Lis had not expected such spine from Madison. Lis felt mean to realize how desperate she thought Madison was, but she certainly did fish attention from people. To rebut someone so firmly sounded so out of her character, especially when it came to Tyler. It was refreshing to hear; maybe she was starting to develop.

"So, are you mad at him though?"

"Ah, no. I'm not angry." Lis's tone was clearly off, as she could feel Silvia cutting her eyes at her from under her lashes.

"Alright, you don't have to tell me anything." Silvia smirked and leaned back into the window, and though Lis knew she was being funny, she also felt desperate to assure Silvia that she was enjoying this way of being questioned. She especially enjoyed that Silvia was not leaving Lis room to ask about her in turn. Though Lis would have been interested in hearing about how Silvia's life was going, she was thriving on the knowledge that Silvia was reaching out to her. She would not feel so special if it were anyone else, but Silvia's attention acted like a tonic, perhaps because her impressively stacked schedule made time with her so rare and her words sound so sure.

"It's not that, I just don't know how much you want to hear."

"I'm not squeamish."

Lis rolled things around in her head, but only a little bit. She had only been waiting for someone to turn on the taps. "I just think that, in one aspect, I might have moved too fast."

"Fucking?"

"Yes."

"Did he hurt you?" The way Silvia turned to look at her, like she was ready to help Lis in whatever way she needed, almost made Lis wish she *had* been hurt somehow, but that was a grim thing to playact. "No no no, it was just—honestly it was just bad. And after, I felt so... slimy. Like I was just sloshing around, like—"

"You make it sound like you were about to prolapse."

"Gross."

"Usually '*slimy*' is not quite a bad thing, in context. Did any of it feel good?"

"Like thirty seconds of it, but not enough."

"Yeah that's really not enough." Silvia let a silence brew for a moment while she blew out a little more smoke. One of the apartments across the way dimmed its recessed kitchen lighting. "Well, the first one is usually not great, but it can get better."

This, Lis knew, since with Ty, it had been leagues better. Getting to come was one part of it, but more than that, the slimy feeling didn't return. Sleeping with Ty was invigorating. It made her feel both powerful and peaceful. Lis didn't respond for a while; Silvia kept glancing at her. It was too jerky of a movement for someone who should have been stoned, but it made sense when Silvia spoke again. With a husky, heavy voice, she said, "You can tell me."

She knew, but instead of embarrassed, Lis felt relieved. She even laughed a little, from the release of nerves. "How did you know?"

"Well, obviously it was Trevor. And you *should* be mad at him, because that was not his business, but he only told me because it would be unrealistic for him to keep a secret from me, and he knows I wouldn't be an asshole about it."

"Well, is that true?"

"Oh of course, don't worry about it. I mean, I like Tyler, he's a very sweet boy, but you don't seem like a bad person so I figure you must have a good reason. And like, if it were someone who was just like Tyler, maybe I'd be a little judgemental, but it's not like that."

"What do you mean?"

"I mean—Ty is a lot different than Tyler. He's got different things to offer, so it's not like you're fucking him to be greedy. Not greedy in *that* sense, anyway."

"You know Ty?"

Silvia nodded her head deeply. "I know Ty."

"You *know* Ty?"

"Yep."

Lis's instinct was not to be jealous, which made her proud of herself. Actually, it felt good that someone who'd sleep with Silvia would also want to sleep with her. She also realized that she now had an opportunity.

"So, what was it like for you?"

"It was great! He's good, he's cute, and he's funny. And he wasn't annoying afterward. There's not a lot of people I've gotten to revisit, because they get the wrong ideas, you know. But even now when I see him, he's a friend."

"But how did it compare with other people?"

"Well everyone's different. He has ways he likes to do things, I have mine, and where those overlap is what makes it good or not."

This did and didn't make sense to Lis. There was a logic so simple in Silvia's statement that it must be true, but it didn't feel like an answer to Lis's question. Both Ty and Tyler had been in touch with hidden parts of her, but to be with Tyler felt like hosting a foreign body, and with Ty it felt like a welcome.

It didn't really matter what the particulars were, but even then, both men had penetrated her, kissed her, touched her. She explained this to Silvia.

"Well, Ty's done it more, so he's better at it, and he probably talked to you differently."

"Right. He did."

Lis was waiting for Silvia to say something that would explain why her night with Ty had left an explosion in its wake, but she realized that for Silvia, it simply hadn't been that big a deal. Lis looked out at the skyline. She leaned her face further into the window, and wished that she could stick her head out, but she would have caught her head in the security bars. "I'm going to break up with Tyler," she said. It was the first time she said it out loud, and she felt how much she meant it. "Of course you are," said Silvia. She continued, "and then what?"

"Who knows." Lis could have said more, she could have said that she would pursue Ty once Tyler was out of the picture. But she didn't. Why could she take one step and not the other? She considered the words she'd said, and waited for more to come out of her mouth, but they didn't.

2017

Ty had never deleted Tinder from his phone. He kept it as a way of signaling to anyone who might be looking over his shoulder that he had not entirely given up on dating. And yet, it had been ages since he'd scrolled through for matches. His profile was dated, he had new tattoos not featured in his photos, and his hair was marginally better now. His profile read "looking for someone to stare out of windows and pet dogs with." He'd never been especially creative. There was no note indicating that he was trans on his profile, instead, he made sure to feature a photo of himself with his scars out and visible. In those old photos, he looked happier. When he was actually using the app, the few dates he went on had not been strained by the need to come out. The girls who matched with him never gave him any indication that they'd clocked him, and it ended up not mattering when the night ended with neither party extending the offer to host.

Ty was so sick of being alone, and so aware that he had no one but himself to blame. He tried to remind himself that he was, indeed, attractive. He got out of bed, walked to his mirror, and took a few shots of himself, trying his best to balance the self-awareness of a mirror selfie with a mix of self-deprecating shame and allure. The photos came out with him looking lost. He deleted them and opened Tinder, didn't update a single element of his profile, apart from the age range he was looking within, and began swiping. The landscape had changed from how he remembered it. There were a lot more interesting people on the app then there had been before, and he found himself intimidated in a way he had never been. This was a hard blow, to realize that he could not so easily resume being the flirt he used to be. Years of solitude had made him shy. The girls in his phone flew past him in improbably-colored outfits, all of them seemed to possess an internal sundial that told them exactly where to stand for a photo such that the sun would light them up perfectly. Silvia came up in the mix; that she was dating men again was something he'd deal with later. It was highly likely that she would never expect him to return to the swiping game and he was not meant to see this. For a moment he did consider swiping right on her profile (he could play it off as a joke between friends if he needed to), but thoughts of Lita stopped him. Then again, for all he knew, she was in the mix as well with her markers set to "women only."

After twenty minutes of lefts, he found a right swipe, though it took him several minutes of deliberation to work up the courage. The girl, Madison, was like a ghost from the past. He didn't need to see the labels on her clothes to know they came exclusively from H&M and Forever 21. Her photos, like his, looked dated, but based on elements of the scenery behind her he knew they must have been taken recently. Her profile read "Marketing MA! Class of 2020! Lifelong theater geek (talk to me about how *you* defy gravity)! Looking for someone who can handle my craziness and share his with mine!" She seemed unbearable, but she was pretty and probably nice. Something about her hair falling flat against her head and the fake pearls in her ears took him back to an aborted life he once wanted with unfair desperation. As soon as he swiped right, he started sweating so much he put his phone down. He immediately began to hope that they wouldn't match. Anxiety held him in a vice grip for all of eight minutes until his phone lit up with a notification that they had matched. Madison's first message was punctuated with glitter emojis. She called him "cutie" in greeting. Though still sweating and pathetic, he was relieved to find that this kind of treatment still did something for him. He tried to resurrect the parts of his old self that knew what to say to compel girls to him, and felt a bit sick for it. As he saw his own words popping up in right-aligned bubbles between her messages (she seemed reluctant to use one text for her whole message, instead sending several bubbles at a time as if the shapes that held her words were their own punctuation), he could hear them in a voice that sounded more like his brother's than his. In order to continue, he told himself that this was just a no-stakes bit of practice. *Sorry Madison*, he thought. But to remain fair to her, he didn't completely prohibit the thought of this being his potential soulmate from entering his head. When she suggested a rooftop bar in midtown for their first meeting, he knew this was doomed, but he accepted the invitation anyway. If not now, when?

Madison moved fast, which he didn't necessarily love, but it at least kept him from stewing in his nerves for too long. She wanted to meet him the very next night, and since he now had an email job, there was nothing stopping him from going. He wondered if she was the type of person to be more offended by his offering to pay than not.

When she arrived in an outfit that appeared to be the same exact one from her profile photos, he thought he might be being pranked. As much as he tried to scrape together a healthy font of self-esteem, he was not able to believe that he'd matched with someone—even someone he wasn't that interested in,—and that he was actually outside, about to go on a date. He wondered, was this was trans insecurity or regular insecurity? "It's so nice to meet you!" She said when she arrived, and she gave him the European-style double cheek kisses to say hello. "You too," he replied. The way he was smiling and the tone of his voice was precisely what he used in the office. In fact, the clothes he was wearing were work clothes; his little blue button-up and black pants. Only his shoes were normal. The outfit made him a little self-conscious, but Madison's clothes also looked like the kind of thing someone in a marketing department would wear. Remembering that she was a grad student, he guessed that she was the "dress for the job you want" type.

Madison had been to this bar before, probably with other dates. She guided him to a table with a view of the city, and as they drank he saw her looking at him in ways that reminded him of the past. She talked about her schooling, how she'd gotten her undergraduate degree in theater and was now compensating for that "unrealistic" degree with something more practical. Ty wanted to know how she had gotten into a marketing program with a theater undergrad, but it would have been rude to scrutinize. She was very pretty, and she talked so fast that he didn't have to do very much. With regret, he realized that he was hoping to sense something familiar, like the smell of doll plastic, the way Lis smelled. That spoiled his night, especially as traces of Madison's gaze made him feel a bit too seen. She acted like she knew him from somewhere. The effect it gave was as if he was being haunted. He kept his composure, and Madison seemed to have a good time. She lived nearby, and asked him to walk her home, which of course he would.

At her door, she paused on the step with her keys. "Do you want to come up?" Ty felt strange, not only because he hadn't expected her to be so forward, but because he was now in a position where he was certain that he wanted to say no. Not only that, but his lack of desire wasn't just because he didn't feel a connection. Madison's offer and her skirt brought him memories; not of two years ago, but just a few weeks ago. He could feel Nat's hand on the back of his neck as if he were right in front of him. Horrified, he recognized that what he was feeling was an excess of satisfaction. Even if he and Madison hadn't clicked, they could still have hooked up, that was what Tinder was built for, but he was good.

When Ty got home, it was quiet. He decided that he no longer enjoyed the silence. Max's door was open and the light off, and no light shone through the crack at the bottom of the bathroom door. She wasn't home. Nat's door was closed, his room probably getting stuffy and full of stale air. The drinks Ty had had with Madison were making him feel a bit free. Before he knew it, his hand was on Nat's doorknob, his still-shod foot crossing the threshold. He quickly pulled off his shoes so as not to be rude. He turned on a lamp, illuminating the many prints taped to Nat's walls. They were mostly big blocks of text; Ty recognized the familiar lines of "I Want a Dyke for President." He was surprised, since Nat made a big deal about not using slurs. Then, he saw the latter half of "Litanies to my Heavenly Brown Body." Then, of course, Lou quotes. Nat had, in pencil, scribbled several in his shitty handwriting on post-its and pressed them to the wall. Some had fallen to the floor in the weeks he'd been gone. Ty nearly stepped on "I want to look like what I am but don't know what someone like me looks like." He was surprised that he hadn't noticed any of this when he'd last been in here, because now that he was paying attention, it was like the walls of this room were chanting at him. He saw a few books on Nat's desk, ones that Lita had been trying to get Ty to read ever since he'd met her. Not only that, but Nat had stuffed each one full of post-it flags. They all looked finished; if there was one Nat was in the middle of, it was probably keeping him company while he lay in a twin bed somewhere in Jersey stripping his drains. Despite himself, Ty got a bit emotional.

He'd never spent much time in this room. The roommate before Nat kept it sealed; the longest time he'd been in here, he'd been preoccupied. Ty approached the desk where Nat read his books, and sat. The window Nat had pushed the desk against was fairly large. Ty would have been jealous if he didn't have the fire escape to himself. He looked through the glass. The crack in the alley below was getting wider. Some long strands of grass grew out of it. They were breaking through just in time to catch a little fresh air before winter. Looking at the view of the alley he had from Nat's window, Ty realized something. As he lifted his gaze, his suspicions were confirmed. Nat's window looked directly at Ty's fire escape.

14

2015

Now that Silvia knew, there was no need to fear going to the bars on nights when she was there. A door had opened, an expanse broadened, and the two halves of Lis's life were closer to meeting. Dancing with Silvia, bouncing between her and Trevor—against whom Lis didn't hold a grudge; on "confronting" him about his loose lips, they both only laughed, and he'd hugged her so closely, apologizing profusely, and she could only feel grateful to him—and Ty, she felt lightheaded. She'd never been high before, but this was what she'd always imagined it was like. Lis felt more awake than she ever had, she could feel the pretense of a sore throat from talking to so many people. People were approaching her, making room in their conversations for her, brushing her hands and asking her to dance. If she weren't so euphoric she could have cried. And yet, there was still something. Like a grain of hard rice stuck in her throat, there was a needly little pinprick. It could have been fear, it could have been sadness, but whatever it was, it was small and—in that moment —weak enough that she could tamp it down for the night.

As Lis watched Silvia dancing, seeing her in the bar for the first time since she and Trevor had first taken them all there just a few months ago, she felt her attachment to discretion weaken. Silvia and Ty talked, and when she spoke to him he laughed and was clearly charmed, but he always returned to look at Lis. When they saw each other, he gave her attention that he didn't give to anyone else. It was like he was throwing her a rope she could take or leave as she wished. He didn't seem like the type to *need* a girlfriend, but he would appreciate it if one showed herself to him. The day she spent with him at his apartment was lovely, but she was eager to be alone with him. Lis crossed the bar, and slipped her hand behind his back. "What if we left a little early?" She asked. She wanted to be as clear as she could while still maintaining some level of flirtation, and she wanted to see if he would reject her. He didn't.

Perhaps she should have set a limit for herself, a promise that after one time, she'd stop. But to do so would only be to keep up the pretense that she was taken, and Lis no longer thought of herself that way. She knew she wasn't single, but she knew that she would be soon, and what she had with Ty was much more substantial than anything she had with Tyler. Besides, Tyler was a simple, attractive boy. He had been fine before Lis and would be after her. She'd already imagined a near future in which she would be confronted with his new girlfriend and could gracefully say hello to her, maybe even be friends. She knew Tyler had served his purpose. Having hardly seen him since the scene presentations, she got to thinking that by the time she broke it off, he might have even forgotten they were dating.

Ty called them a car. Once at his building, she walked up the few floors to his unit, getting a pleasant flush along the way. Ty unlocked the door and led her to his room in a few short movements. They flirted for a few minutes, and then they had their mouths pressed together. When she leaned into him, she felt an ease and a resistance, like he was accepting what she had for him and giving back something of his own. She wanted everything he had. They ended up in a similar position to how they'd started last time, with her under him and his hand between her legs. This time though, she felt bold. She reached into his pants, hoping to get clues from his response that would tell her how he wanted to be touched. He gasped, but he didn't push her away. and the clues she hoped for didn't come, but her guesses got plenty of enthusiasm.

She'd never gone down on anyone before. She began to sit up, and he followed her lead, rolling over to let her get on top of him, but she didn't stay there for long. She did what she thought would be sexy from movies, kissing him down his neck until she got to his crotch, then pulling down his pants and underwear in one go. If being touched like this bothered him, he had an odd way of showing it. The noises he made, and the knowledge that she was responsible for them gave Lis the confidence she needed to try something she'd never done before. She could tell he was surprised when he reached out a hand as if to stop her, but when she looked at him to see if she'd done something wrong, he let his arm fall and his eyes softened as he nodded at her to keep going. From her vlog-watching habits, she knew to be gentle, and more importantly she knew what to expect when he was naked. His was not the first trans dick she'd ever seen, but it was the first one she'd ever seen in person. The motion of her mouth came naturally, this was quite possibly the easiest thing she'd ever done. To imagine herself in Ty's position and imagine what he would want was like second nature, and she was pleased to learn that it made her feel good too. Her jaw did get tired after some minutes, but she didn't stop until he came.

She crawled up to lay next to him and watch him catch his breath, feeling her own exertion as a mirror of his. He had little to say except "fuck," and leaned into her. She knew they'd get back to her at some point, but for now she was content to lay with him, leaning her head on his chest and listening to his lungs. She ran her hand over his chest, admiring its warmth. She traced his ribs from the bottom up, counting one, two, three, four, and five, until she got to the plum-colored scars that ran towards each other and stopped short of meeting a few inches shy of his sternum. When she touched the scars, he shivered, then explained, "Sorry, that's not you, these aren't that old and the sensation is still weird." It was odd to Lis to think of the scars being relatively new. Of course it made sense now. Ty worked at a cafe; if he had health insurance, it likely didn't cover a surgery like this, and it must have taken him years to save up for it. The cheapest surgeon she knew of charged $6,000, but ones local to the city usually charged more like $10-$12k. Lis had done food service summer jobs back home, a surgery like that would eat up half a year's income, and Ty had to support himself to boot. "It must be such a relief," she said. "You can't imagine." She could, though. Feeling uninhibited, she took the risk of asking a question that she might normally worry about being invasive: "Do the binders hurt?" He looked at her for a second, and she worried that she'd offended him, but then he got up—slowly, she was pleased to note the unsteadiness in his walk that was her doing—and plucked something off the shelf in his closet.

"Here." He passed her a limp looking half-shirt, stretchy on one side, meshy on the other. "Why don't you try it?"

It was a binder, one Ty didn't need anymore but kept for some reason. Sentimentality? His gaze at her had no mischief, he wasn't testing her, only trying to answer her question. What better way to find out than to just try it herself?

"Okay."

She examined the binder. It was worn in, Ty must have used this one every day. It was a shade nearly the same as her skin, but darkened around the neck and armpits. It seemed like no big deal, just put it on like a sports bra, she thought. But when she put her arms through and let the binder fall around her head, she realized her mistake. The thing was like a heavy-duty rubber band. The binder was around Lis's face and biceps, she couldn't figure out how to get her arms down. Ty stepped in to make sure she didn't asphyxiate herself.

With the binder on, Lis's chest was perfectly smooth, but not quite as flat as she'd been hoping. Her chest made a slight convex dome over her ribs a few centimeters tall. Nothing one would notice under a sweater. "Yeah, I figured you're about the same size I was," Ty said. "That one is pretty old, so it's given up a little, when you get a new one it's much tighter." The binder wasn't painful the way Lis expected, but she could see how this could get frustrating. She could breathe, but that last sip of air she expected from a nice deep breath was thwarted. It wouldn't kill her, but it wasn't satisfying. The straps dug into her shoulder, and she could imagine what this must feel like in the summer.

Still, she liked wearing it. It made her feel comforted, like she was being held in. The feeling was like reassurance. "It looks good on you," Ty said as he leaned in to kiss her. The kiss made Lis feel like her brain had just come on for the first time. He continued to kiss her, and repeated what she'd done to him, moving his lips down her neck, her stomach, until he was kneeling in front of her. Lis watched his hair move while his face was buried in between her legs. Her panting was exaggerated by the binder, and for a moment as she came she did worry that she might not be able to breathe, but the fear passed quickly and was replaced by a lightheadedness that made her fall back on the bed.

Afterwards, they lay mixed up in each other, talking as if nothing had happened, but with a sincerity in the air that felt comforting. She looked at her hand on his belly, the white hand on white skin in distinct but nearby shades. How narrow a slice of life this was, how limited. They got drowsy, and it became clear Lis would be spending the night. Ty pointed out that she shouldn't fall asleep with the binder on, so she let him help her take it off. They continued talking, and with every slight pause in the conversation she looked at him with purpose. Behind her eyes, something in her waved around a flag to get attention. She stared, and the thing was frantic, begging Ty to notice, wanting him to pull it out, embarrass it if necessary. Anything to get it born.

2017

Lita and Silvia did not yet live together, but Lita was at Silvia's often enough that if Ty wanted to see either of them, he just needed to find a good time to go to the studio in Gowanus where Silvia stationed herself between dance classes. Lita wanted them to live together, but not until they could afford to rent one of those apartments on Eastern Parkway that took up the whole floor of what used to be a single-family house. Silvia's apartment was small and seemed to have too many corners for a studio, but it allowed her to live without roommates, and the super obeyed fire code and left the roof door unlocked. Therefore, when Ty was over to see Lita, they went up above the building for some air and to give Silvia some space. Ty's own building had a frieze that gave the roof a three-foot wall on all sides, but up on Silvia's there were spaces and gaps where one could just fall off. The roof had a single lawn chair, where Lita sat; the chair was not hers, its provenance was a mystery. Ty sat on the ground next to her while she smoked. That evening, he looked up at the trail from her cigarette that wove a lace around her head and asked, "can I have one?"

"You're gonna cough," she said.

"I'm not gonna cough, I used to smoke all the time."

She looked at him like a big sister would, willing and perhaps eager to let him get into trouble. "Alright."

After a drag, Ty's eyes watered while he held back an itch in his throat. He'd come up here seeking some relief. A jog; an emotional TBI. He'd felt trapped in his head lately, as if there were a little cop in there, bashing in all the impulses that would let him enjoy a single thing in life. Sleeping with Nat had awoken all kinds of dissatisfaction he hadn't realized he was harboring; his loneliness, the job he had that had been such a goal for so long but was still the lowest rung of a ladder he couldn't see the top of, the way he felt like he was drifting from one place to another without any of the breeziness that detachment is supposed to connote. He was a monorail, not a boat.

Lita looked at his flushing face. "Honey, cough." Ty looked back at her, wondering why she was his friend. Lita and Silvia and Max, his favorite friends. They'd all picked him, but Lita was unique in that she'd met him after the event that Silvia and Max blamed for making him so uptight, which Ty had come to interpret as their gentle way of telling him he was less fun than he used to be. Ty coughed, satisfied by the breakup in his throat, and Lita didn't laugh at him. He stubbed the cigarette into the roof tar and handed her the remnant to save for later. She screwed up her eyes as if to study him, and began to start a conversation he could contribute to.

"I think Silvia wants another girlfriend. Like, in addition to me, not instead of."

Ty raised his eyebrows. "A sharing girlfriend?"

"I don't need another one, so if the offer was on the table I wouldn't take it."

"Are you okay with that?" Ty knew that Lita and Silvia fucked around, but he didn't think it was in the polyamorous way. They were open, and each seemed secure enough in each other that they didn't have any qualms about the side-fucking, with Ty assuming that they were the kind of couple to generously negotiate such things. Lita's shoulders, sloping around her chest as if she had wings to shelter herself with, told another story.

She took another drag of her cigarette. "I don't know. I think it would depend on the girlfriend."

Ty let things be quiet for a minute. He had an unfair

knee-jerk reaction; he couldn't help but draw a line between Silvia and Nat's close friendship and their wanting to have two relationships at once. But Silvia was an adult, and one of his most dependable friends, and Nat's duplicity was old news. The circumstances did not at all compare, and Ty's realization of the degree to which he'd let his brain become hot-wired for bitterness made him a bit sick. To cut off his own thoughts, he said "I didn't know you were so commitment-oriented."

"I'm not, but I love her."

Ty didn't know what to say, didn't know what sort of advice to give or if it was wanted. Instead, he felt like it was his turn; Lita brought up her troubles to level the playing field. It was one of her kindest traits, the way that she did not make friends feel like they were in a confessional. Ty appreciated the reminder that his problems were not the only problems. Yet he was at a loss for where to begin, or what he hoped Lita could give him.

"You know what happened with me and Nat?" He assumed Silvia had probably told Lita about his and Nat's hook-up.

"Not the whole story, but Nat and Silvia have given me the basics."

"Oh, I meant... Um." Ty felt a little tricked. He'd hadn't meant to tell the *whole* story, in his own words. He'd never done it before. It hadn't been necessary, all his other friends had been there. It dawned on him that with how much he liked Lita it might be unfair that she'd never heard the story from him. He knew that Nat and Silvia's takes would have hit different beats, emphasizing things that didn't matter to him as much, or including things he didn't know. He had some vague knowledge of how things had broken down for Nat back then, something about dorm drama because of some friend of the boyfriend who was also Nat's roommate. Ty could only speak for himself, and he began to. He told Lita about the very first time he met Nat, about being attracted and confused by the apparent straight girl who was clearly nervous to be in her first gay bar, but somehow not annoying in the way that straight people could be. He told Lita about how the Nat of that era had become his friend, and then about the first time they went to his apartment together. He told Lita about how he thought that maybe a relationship was starting. He told her about how Nat had no questions—without going into too much detail, he talked about how he thought that Nat must have slept with trans guys before, and maybe that was why, despite the nerves, he hadn't been obnoxious at the bar. He told Lita about how they didn't see each other much in the daytime, but how that could have easily been chalked up to Nat's classes and Ty's day job. Then, he told Lita about how it ended, with Nat showing up to his apartment to tell him that he'd had a boyfriend the whole time, but not anymore. He told her about the disorientation of finding out he was a side piece after the relationship had ended, and how he felt compelled to shut Nat out immediately. He told her about how he didn't see Nat for months while his semester ended and he went home to Jersey for the summer. He didn't see Nat again until he was Nat. Silvia had given him a heads up as a way of letting him know that Nat would no longer be cold-shouldered away from the bar. He couldn't be, he belonged there now in the same way that Ty did. When fall came and Nat showed up at one of Max's shows, people were so charmed by him that it became clear to Ty that they'd missed having him around. Unnoticed by Ty, Nat had been making friends besides him at the bar the whole time they'd known each other. Laying a groundwork. His friends had only accepted his absence for Ty's benefit, and now clearly felt the enough time had passed and Ty should be over it.

As he spoke, he recalled the night he'd let Nat try on his old binder. It wasn't that he'd ever forgotten it, but it was like a set piece, a memory that hovered in the background of this story, made insignificant by Ty's subconscious will. He remembered that night, he remembered looking at Nat, naked, and feeling a brain cell twitch, possessing him to pull the binder from his closet and toss it to Nat. After Nat put it on, it felt like they had undressed with each other for the first time. Remembering this while talking to Lita, he left it out of his story. At first because it seemed like unnecessary detail, but as he continued talking, he noticed that he was stumbling over his words, like the tale he was telling was a tower he built as he spoke, and that little detail was a beam that jeopardized the stability of the whole structure. By the time he finished talking, he barely understood the con-clusion he came to. Lita seemed to notice something was off.

"So *this* is why you two are so exhausting about each other?"

Ty looked at her and chewed on the inside of his cheek. "Mm-hmm," he said, betraying a lack of confidence in himself that he hoped Lita would gloss over. She nodded, and let the last few centimeters of her cigarette blow away. She watched it fall to the street. "That'll take someone's eye out, probably." They could have gone back inside, but the sun was setting. As Ty had done after Lita's confession, Lita stayed quiet, not offering any comment or advice, but simply letting the story stretch out in the air. The breeze picked up.

Lita leaned back in her chair. "You ever think about what being trans is?"

"Yeah, all the time."

"Right... but I mean the *definition*. Like, honestly when it all gets too much for me I think about TV, the girl brain boy body thing. Well, the opposite for you."

"Yeah, *Degrassi*."

"Well, maybe you had *Degrassi*, I started with *Twin Peaks*."

"Sorry."

She shrugged. "I'll take David Duchovny over Jordan Todosey actually. Anyway, sometimes I think I'm okay with that logic. I mean, I read theory and all that stuff, and I have a certain appetite for thinking complexly and trying to hold on to a million things in your head, but I need a break sometimes. I feel like at the very least, you can say it's a body thing. A mismatch."

"I get it."

"Like, if I went and got a pussy tomorrow, am I still different? Yeah, but why? I've heard five hundred different answers. 'It's the socialization,' 'it's the history,' 'it's spiritual,' etc. I can pick one, and I *do*, but it feels like there's more to think about than I have time for before I die. And you, I mean you pass all the time, but I don't think you or anyone else could say you're the same as a cis man, right?"

"I hope not."

"Well, cis men aren't always the worst kind of men."

Ty knew this to be true, but rather than harp on it as if he'd never been a bad man, he said, "I think I need to forget sometimes. Like, at this point, all the trans stuff about me is so mundane that I can almost pretend it's not real. And then I have one of those moments where I think about the odds that I could have been anyone else, and how there's not a lot of trans people, and I am one, and it throws me. And then I get upset for some reason, because I feel... I feel like, stupid. Stupid. I don't know what for."

Lita nodded heavily, and grabbed the three-quarter cigarette Ty'd forfeited. "Fuck. I wasn't sad when we came up here."

"Sorry."

"It's fine. You have to have a pity party sometimes. It can't be sexy perverts and bitchiness all the time. Especially when you're alone."

"Right before bed."

"Exactly."

Ty looked behind him to see if there was any obvious trash on the roof. He lay down and pretended the airborne grime of his home didn't settle here every day. Ty wondered what would happen to him after all this; the petty fights, the day to day dramas, the concerns, the pharmacy calls.

Lita looked at him lying on the roof, with no blanket or anything to separate him from the ground. "Your hair is gonna stink."

15

2015

Lis sat on a metal folding chair outside the great hall, waiting to audition for *Spring Awakening*—the play, not the musical, much to the disappointment of many of her classmates. Memorizing her monologue had been easy. The first year she had had to do this, she was penalized for going over the two minute time limit. In the real world, if you offended casting directors by wasting their time with a too-long monologue, you were kicked out, so the school simulated this to prepare students. When you started your monologue, they set an iPhone timer and cut you off when it binged. From her folding chair in the waiting area, Lis compulsively checked her phone out of both boredom and nerves. The scene work with Tyler had left a bad taste in her mouth, one that shook her conviction in her ability to perform. When she was a freshman, her future career was certain, but now it was as if all she'd learned in the past three years was that she was less suited to this line of work than she thought. She had stopped wanting leads. With every audition, she aimed herself in the hope that instead of playing the ingenue, she would be picked for something with more meat, more of an opportunity to surprise. The lead had to shine all the way through, and yet, all the leading women's roles were forgettable. It was the Marthas, Mashas, maids, and schoolteachers that thrilled.

The first audition she nailed was in middle school, when she got to play Jessica in *The Merchant of Venice*. The adults at her school praised her for being able to handle such a mature role, praise they didn't give to the girl playing Portia, and all Lis had had to do was a few scenes and a fake-out kiss at the end. She remembered watching the director (who worked during the days as one of the English faculty) tear into Portia, accusing her of stiffness, woodenness, and "utter undesirability." The director expected the girl to imagine being appealing, even if she didn't feel that way. These were all things Lis was guilty of as well, but her stage time was so limited that she didn't become a target. Her performance had been such a success that the only thing she wanted to forget was the night that, after the audience had left and the cast and crew remained to clean up, the director yanked her into a side hug to give her a kiss on the cheek. At the time, she let it feel like the kind of affection one gets from an uncle, even a compliment.

These auditions took hours. All drama students were required to audition for every play from their second semester onwards. The school might have been small, but the theater majors repre-sented its largest demographic, about 1600 of its 2000 students. To alleviate the crowding, the auditions were held in alphabeti-cal batches, and each student was given a free pass to skip class if it ran through their audition slot. Lis's preparation was min-imal, but devoted. She worked hard on her monologue, drank water, and left it at that. Some of the people around her chose to run scales, or stretch, which never made any sense to her. Trevor told her stories about the MT auditions, which sounded like nightmares. People sang or belted over each other to warm up their throats and took off their shoes to do gymnastics for the muscles. Trevor himself did sun salutations and something called fire breath.

Lis's monologue was from something called *Reasons to be Pretty*. She hated the play, but the monologue suited her type, and she had looked for something easy. She had little faith in her ability to secure a position in the cast after the disaster that was her scene work with Tyler. It wasn't that she felt the disaster represented a failure of her own talents, but rather that this was a small school, and there was a cabal of acting majors who were so successful in their classes that, though the school insisted on a "no-favoritism" policy, the praise thrown upon them by their professors carried heavy influence. Lis had always gotten As and Bs in her acting classes, but she'd never been able to get in good with a professor that could pull strings and get her cast in something. There would not be many opportunities after this.

When Lis was called in to come read for the casting directors, her mind had been on other things. This audition was sure to be a wash, but she wasn't too bothered by it. It had been a long time since she performed on stage, and that feeling was something she missed to be sure, but the semester was ending soon, and that meant freedom was approaching. She was ready to give Tyler the bad news, to tell him that she needed to move on, they were going in different directions, and then she would go home for a few weeks. She imagined making plans to take the train into the city on weekends to see Ty until the break was up and she'd be back in New York full-time. She looked forward to completely letting go of any need to hide. And yet, there was still a part of her that wanted Ty to be a secret. She wasn't ashamed of him,—in fact, she *wanted* to be seen with him—but she wanted the permission secrecy gave her to be someone else when she was alone with him.

Thus, Lis was distracted while giving her monologue. When her name was called, she walked in to stand before a panel of professors who were vaguely familiar with her, if not from classes, then from past auditions. Thankfully, the professor who'd assigned her and Tyler's scene was not on the casting team. Lis's monologue was from the perspective of an attractive woman who is trying to be self-aware of her prettiness and the privileges it gives her, while still being compelled to let her audience know that prettiness invites cruelty in the same way ugliness does. People have desired her, and hated her for it. At the end, she starts talking about her unborn baby girl, and her wish that she'll be pretty, but not more than that. It was very Daisy Buchanan. Before she could finish, a ringtone began to play, and one of the professors' phones flashed "0:00."

"Thank you, you can go." The professor nodded with tight lips; this same woman had given her the boot the previous Spring.

Lis did not respond to being dismissed with any perceptible disappointment. She gave a small smile to the panel of judges, and left. The air she left behind was curtness shaped like politeness. It had gone how she'd expected it to go, and she hoped that having no reaction at all would be the right way to make sure this moment was just a void, but as she put her coat on in the hall she knew that it would be read as ingratitude. As a junior, she should know by now that when the time limit says two minutes, you make sure your delivery does not go over. Never mind that she only had sixteen words left to say, those sixteen words, if she'd gotten a chance to say them, were a sign of disrespect. A waste of the casting directors' time and the time of the other auditioners. They had hundreds of students to see. Of course, they wouldn't have to see so many if the auditions weren't mandatory. Lis hadn't been irritated until now, but now she was forced to remember that this was her aspiration. To be at this school was a goal, to graduate was a goal, to apply her training and translate it into a sustainable career was something she wanted. Sometimes she forgot, and the remembrance came at the worst times.

After graduation, her whole life would be striving for auditions like these. Auditioning hadn't gone well for her since high school; it was a wonder to her that she hadn't been pulled aside by anyone in the theater department yet to ask her if she was sure she didn't want to change majors. But what else should she do? There was nothing else she particularly excelled at. Her grades had always been good, but not exemplary. Performing was her life, and she did love it, when given the chance. Maybe she just hadn't been on a stage in a long time. She needed some sort of outlet to remind her what it felt like to have her shades appreciated. As Lis walked to the exit, her boots made hollow noises on the tile. It was a very well-built school. She remembered touring with her parents and feeling so sure that this would be the place where she really came into her element. Instead, the feeling she hoped for, that had eluded her in all the time she'd spent going to classes and bombing auditions, came to her elsewhere. Dancing with Silvia at the bar, breathing in Ty's secondhand smoke, leaning into Trevor when they were both fading drunk and finding sweetness in each other. She wasn't sure if anything was going on that night, but she felt compelled to get on the train and pick a stop off the bridge. But no, she had things to do at home, and besides, it was getting so terribly cold out.

2017

From the street, Ty could look across the water and see two bright pillars of light sticking up out of lower Manhattan. It was officially September, and all day Ty's co-workers had been sharing stories in poor taste, trying to valorize their behavior on a day in which they truly had not mattered much at all. Nat was due home that evening. Max wanted to plan something cute to welcome him, but she'd ended up having to work. Since the weren't speaking, Ty had no idea when to expect him. Once in the door, he looked around for signs of activity. There was a lamp on that he was fairly certain Max wouldn't have left before her shift, being that she'd left the apartment in the afternoon. Within a few minutes, Ty spotted a dried-out umbrella propped up against his door. When he went to examine it, he heard a voice behind him.

"I realized when I opened it on the way to the train."

This was a lie. Ty was the only person in the apartment who had a working umbrella, so on the day he'd left, Nat would have picked it up, maybe thinking of it as a subtle petty gesture, then committing to the slight as he walked under its protection for a few blocks. He might have dreaded this interaction on coming back, and Ty thought about why he'd chosen to plop it at Ty's door rather than wordlessly leaving it in the hallway where he'd found it. If he wanted to, Nat could have easily convinced Ty he'd never taken it, that Ty had just spent weeks having lost track of this item, and Ty wouldn't have had many options other than believe him or pick a fight. Tricking him into picking a fight was the kind of thing Ty was given to expect from Nat, but now, looking at his sorry/surly face and the flaccid umbrella on the floor, he felt a pinprick emotion, realizing again that he was needlessly ungenerous when it came to his many assumptions about Nat. Now that Nat was back home, it was like Ty was re-living the growth of his bitterness. Without Nat, he'd spent the past few weeks thinking about what he could do differently, what might make their shared home a little easier to live in, if Nat chose to stay.

Maybe if Ty broke himself down a bit, let go of some things, he could be re-shaped or returned to his old self. Then again, that would be the self that brought Nat into his life in the first place. Maybe it was him, the unburdened Ty, who came up for air the previous month on that very hot August night.

The umbrella smelled of dried up mineral deposits. Ty looked from it to Nat, and spotted the trim outlines of the mandatory post-op binder under the ill-fitting button-down he wore. There was a part of Ty that wanted to see Nat's results. He wanted the shirt to open and the binder to unravel so that he could see what it all looked like. He realized that he was hoping for confirmation that it had all been worth it.

In the time that had passed since Ty and Nat slept together, things and thoughts long buried in Ty had expressed themselves like an acne purge. He was becoming disgusted with himself, and experienced a level of self-loathing he used to be well-acquainted with. He was sinking in distress; he remembered just a few months ago, when he felt like he was settled, in a manner of speaking. It had been a period in which no obstacles were due to be thrown at him. Back then he'd thought, *maybe this is a plateau. Maybe from here on out my problems will be somewhat average.* He'd imagined work stress, car trouble, loneliness. It now seemed that that was a naive illusion he'd tricked himself into thinking was sustainable. And besides, it wasn't as if he was satisfied then. Satisfaction, he knew, was not the same as happiness. Happiness was wholly unsustainable and defined by luck. Satisfaction was slightly better than contentment, in that it belied more pleasure and fewer troubles, but still should be more manageable to come by in comparison to happiness. And yet, here he was, staring down a body in front of him that he knew to be good and warm, and yet feeling an awful sickness at just the thought of reaching out while sober.

Nat stood and glanced between Ty and various objects in the room for a while, then turned and went back to his corner of the apartment. Ty realized he hadn't said thank you, nor otherwise acknowledged the return of the umbrella; he'd unwittingly played the part of petulant silent treatment observer. Another little bullet point for his list of things to hate about himself.

The things Silvia and Lita told him weighed on him every day. Silvia had pointed out some problems he'd either missed or ignored, and Lita had given him hope, but not too much, and not in a way that was necessarily uplifting. Aside from their rooftop session, Lita helped him in another, unexpected way. The faith that she put in Nat, or perhaps the benefit of doubt she gave him, was comforting. He wondered where Lita's store of empathy for Nat came from. Ty always thought of her as having a mean edge he didn't; maybe he had been unfair to both of them, and foolish in considering himself. Though he knew he should be working towards not comparing himself to Nat on every count, he was comforted that Lita—and Silvia too, to an extent—believed Nat was, at his core, worth befriending. His annoyances, his contrived opinions, his general greenness and misapprehended sense of humor were faults deemed not too concerning. Growing pains. Was it a forgiveness Nat necessarily deserved? The answer did not matter so much as did the fact that there were people as good as Lita out there who thought so.

Nat re-emerged from his room with his wallet. "I got my birth certificate while I was over there and ended up using some of my savings." He began to pull cards out of the wallet. "Look," he said. Ty did, and saw the driver's license in Nat's hand, one that showed his glowing blond head beside the name, Nathaniel T. Olsson. He braced himself for the middle initial to stand for some bullshit, like Thor. "T?" He asked. "My grandpa's name was Thomas. He was nice to me." Looking closer at the ID, Ty couldn't help but laugh a little. "Did you make your initials N.O. on purpose?" He asked. Nat smiled back, and said, "Yours are T.W., jackass." It was true, Ty hadn't bothered to take his father's surname, Wacek, out of the equation when changing his name. It felt good to laugh with Nat, but the laugh evaporated quickly, and Ty took a step towards his bedroom. "Congratulations," he said, without looking back.

"Hey." Ty turned around in response to Nat's call.

"Yeah?"

Nat looked at Ty earnestly. He still held the ID card in his hand, the one that, despite their tension, he'd been excited to show him. "Is this how it's always going to be with you? Because I still like everything about you that I always have, and I don't hold it against you when talking to you makes me feel like shit, but if you're always going to be like this I want to know if I'm wasting my time."

Ty didn't know what to say. What did he do all day, besides wallow? Silvia had been right, something in him was disconnected, his body was no longer capable of living the life his mind could create. He knew he could be better than this, and had been. Why was he like this now? A jilted lover. That wasn't him, and he knew it. He could care less about some standard-issue straight guy theater kid competing with him. No, it was unfair to act as though Lis had actually hurt him with that. He remembered a night two years ago, a dance party on one of the bar nights that didn't belong to Max, back when there was a scheme to keep Nat's secret under wraps and thus on any night Silvia was there, Nat wouldn't be. Ty remembered an obliterated Trevor mumbling little words about a boy with nearly the same name as Ty, a boy that Nat was dating in name only. However, Ty couldn't remember if he believed it then, because he carried on as if he hadn't heard anything. And then, when it came from Nat's mouth, he'd thrown a tantrum. Thinking on it again, it wasn't the boyfriend that ever made a difference, what upset him was that Nat was confessing, and Ty feared that one confession would beget another. There was something Ty never wanted to learn about Nat, but that he knew would come inevitably.

He remained silent, and eventually Nat gave up on waiting for a response, instead choosing to rustle around the apartment, re-acquainting himself with its clutter. As Ty saw Nat gingerly move about, keeping his elbows close to his body, he understood that he could never have stopped Nat, nor could he have ever inspired him.

16

2015

Cold air helped Lis with many things. Headaches, nerves, stomachaches. Heating pads and warm compresses only made her sweat, but a breeze was good for her. Despite the cold, she chose to walk back to the dorms after her audition. There was no snow on the ground, but there were plenty of frozen crosswalk puddles that forced her to either leap or swerve. It was a good walk, and by the time she got home her heart was beating, making her feel exerted and purged. Lis entered her dorm, oblivious to the stiffness in the air around her. She walked straight into the bedroom, and had not yet put her things down before she was followed in by Madison. Lis could feel Madison's glowing hot face behind her, spoiling the refreshment of her walk. When Lis turned to face her, Madison had a spirit in her neck that reminded Lis of her mother.

"What do you have to say for yourself?" She said, rolling her head around on her neck in a way Lis assumed had been appropriated from the *Bring it On* franchise.

"Excuse me?"

"I know, Lis." Madison looked like she'd spent the better part of the last hour rehearsing her delivery. The effort of carrying around all the imagined weight of her knowledge made her face splotchy. Looking at her, Lis felt the patience she usually reserved for Madison's antics vanish, as if it had been zapped off the earth by a lightning bolt. She narrowed her eyes. "What do you think you know?"

"Last night, Trev and Silvia passed out on the couch when they got home. I got up in the middle of the night, and I asked where you were. Trevor said 'at what's his name's place' and I just figured he was being mean, talking about Tyler. But Tyler wasn't with you, he texted me this morning that all night he'd been going over his audition monologue and went to bed."

For someone so obsessed with Silvia, Lis couldn't believe Trevor mistook Madison's voice for hers. If that was even the case and Trevor hadn't just been tired of keeping other people's secrets. Lis put on the most exasperated face she could come up with. This was one of the practical applications of her acting skill, she could conjure any emotion she needed. With a beleaguered voice, she asked, "What are you trying to say Madison?"

"You're cheating on Tyler!" Madison popped her eyes ou of her head for emphasis, as if her shriek hadn't done the job.

From the living room, a weak but excited voice, Trevor's voice, reached her and Madison, "*OOP!*" It sounded like he was still drunk, and Lis only just became aware that he was still in her dorm. Was Silvia home too? Was everyone here to see this? She took a moment to turn her face towards the door and call out, "Shut up, Trevor," in less of a scold and more of an appeal. She didn't think she had the right to be angry at him. He had been a good friend, letting her into his world and keeping her secrets. Her own ability to do so was harder to hold onto every day. For the first time in her life, she was finding it difficult to lie.

Madison's voice cracked, and she pointed at Lis the way her aunts used to when they took it upon themselves to discipline their sister's kids. "You're gonna tell him."

"You don't even know what you're talking about, Trevor was probably drunk out of his mind, and half asleep."

"It's true!" Trevor called from the couch.

Madison's finger stayed pointed at Lis's chest, unflinching. Lis rolled her eyes. "Why don't you just ask me where I was last night?"

Madison readjusted herself and crossed her arms. "Fine. Where were you last night?"

Lis wanted to be spiteful. She'd defended Madison behind her back as long as they'd known each other, though Madison had given her few reasons to. And now this? Madison wanted to scold her for infidelity? Lis never believed that Madison's hawkishness was motivated by a secret lust for Tyler, but she was simply so annoyed that the only words she could think of were uselessly mean insults, so though she'd fully intended to answer, she could not look into Madison's narrow roseatic face and give her what she wanted. She held her tongue, and wanted to shut the door, but her bedroom was Madison's bedroom, and they were both crammed into it, proof that the space only had standing room for one, as any arrangement of multiples became adversarial.

"Let me out."

She did not push Madison to get out, but she did menace

past. Madison flapped her arms around at no one, as if to say "can you believe this?" Lis walked out the front door with no intention of going anywhere. The hallway was at least a little bit colder than the dorm, and though it was stagnant, the air calmed her down. She intended to spend ten to twenty minutes out here to decompress, hopefully giving Madison enough time to calm down. Maybe then she could head back in and go to bed early, but she wasn't sure there was a comfortable way to sleep in the same room as Madison. For now, Lis was heated and didn't want to think much. In her irritated state, the time went by quickly. After some deep breaths, she went back in, noticing now that Trevor was a limp pile on the couch, and Silvia was gone. Madison sat on the very edge of the couch, as if Trevor were contagious. She was subdued, but the phone clutched in her hand lit up the sustained redness in her face.

"I told him."

From his pile, Trevor spat, "Oh good, maybe now he'll let you breastfeed him." Madison didn't respond, but her lips crinkled. Lis looked at the two of them with tired eyes and said, "Just go back to sleep, Trevor."

They both stayed quiet. Lis held eye contact with Madison, hoping to make her uncomfortable and ashamed of herself. The bedroom was empty now, and she took advantage of the opening to get what she wanted twenty minutes ago. She shut the bedroom door behind her and changed into pajamas. She wished she were at Ty's. She didn't feel like getting her computer, so she pulled out her phone and hooked up her headphones. In her little blanket cave, she logged into her secret email to check her YouTube subscriptions. There was a lot of Christmas-themed content. The guys she'd been following for years put up goofy videos of themselves making cookies and putting together elf costumes for their cats; the newer ones made videos about how to survive the holidays with family, or without. Lis was expected back at her parents' house in just a few weeks. Tyler was going to break up with her. More than anything, it was a relief. She'd hoped it'd happen close to the end of the semester so she could leave all this mess behind. He hadn't tried to call her yet. Maybe he didn't even believe Madison, which would be hilarious. For her to have gone through all the trouble of being vindictive, only for the target of her protection to brush her off, and for Lis to have even bothered to hide her cheating. If he believed Madison and didn't care, it had all been a waste of energy. If he did care, it was still a waste of energy. She should have broken up with Tyler as soon as she met Ty, even if she stood no chance with the latter. Just meeting Ty, becoming part of his world in the small way that she had, was enough for her to know that whatever she wanted, it wasn't Tyler. Lis began to wonder why she hadn't been more open, why she hadn't just pursued Ty openly, unafraid of people like Madison. She now found herself with no romantic options but Ty, and she thought she felt fine. What had she been so scared of?

2017

Ty thought that being a legal adult would make his life easier. To his disappointment, the year he spent being eighteen was spent searching for permission from various entities. Permission from his insurance to go to a therapist, permission from that therapist to get a GID diagnosis, permission from the therapist to accept the life he'd lived till then as satisfaction of the one-year "lived experience" requirement, permission again from the therapist to get a letter saying he met all the requirements, permission from his insurance again to go to an endocrinologist, permission from his endocrinologist to start taking testosterone, permission from his pharmacy to let him use coupons to cover the cost of a vial, permission from his mother to be left in peace, permission from his brother to be left alone, permission from his friends to stay in touch, permission from the internet to start making new friends, and permission from chance to look like a man without having to wait too long. Some requests were granted, others not.

The obstacles were not unexpected, but he'd naively assumed he might be exempt from at least a few of them. Now, he was learning that it was also naive to think that after the initial hurdles, he was done. That after getting the first vial of testosterone, the first binder, the first surgery, etc., he'd be finished. But the firsts were just the firsts. The second vial of T was just as difficult as the first, as was the fifteenth, the thirtieth, and whichever number vial the one he currently needed was. Insurances fucked him over, the cost of the medication got jacked up from $20 to $70, there were needle shortages, and sometimes it seemed his doctor just plain forgot to write his prescription. He didn't know what had happened in this case, only that two and half months since his last shot, he got an unexpected robo-call from the pharmacy letting him know that his prescription was ready for pick-up. He felt like he'd been tossed around in the back of a truck for an hour and then pushed into the street. He did not want to know what the problem had been, and in fact he waited a few days to go pick up his vial because he was scared of going and being met with another issue. But when he showed up at the pharmacy window, they checked him in, gave him his medication, took his $70, and sent him on his way. They even had his preferred 25G needles in stock. He looked into his paper bag of syringes three times before leaving and twice on the train to make sure they were still there.

Back at home in his bedroom he had to psych himself up for the shot, given how long it had been since he'd done it. He forgot to prep a gauze pad, so he had to do an awkward careful shuffle with the syringe sticking out of his belly to get the box from his desk drawer.

Ty was disappointed to find that he still needed his hormones. He'd thought about going off of T as a step to take when he was ready; it seemed the natural progression of things was to take testosterone for so long until all your insufferable traits died out and you assumed a state of glibness that made you attractive and fun. In a way, he was disappointed to be reminded that he needed the drug for a reason. That years on, it was still something he had to participate in. He wasn't ashamed of it at all, but he felt like he should be done by now. The struggle to stay on a medication that did not necessarily keep him alive so much as do something undefinably vital made him feel pathetic, vulnerable, and desperate—and, the current state of things left him unsure of whether his feelings were real or due to lack of T, or a combination of both.

To his mother, he was much the same as a drug addict, like the bodybuilders who abuse anabolic steroids. This was how he knew that his mother thought he was doing all this to gain an advantage, a doping scandal unto himself. Addiction was something he thought about a lot, and now especially so, what with the work it had taken to get this refill. This was a drug that nobody wanted to give him, that required absurd amounts of effort not just to get on but to stay on. What possessed him to work so hard for this? Dysphoria? He often couldn't believe that such a thing was real, and doubted whether he actually felt dysphoric enough to go through all this trouble or if he was just a Munchausen's case. This feeling was compounded the day or two right after his shot, when he felt like the bolts of Zeus coursed through his body. Was that euphoria or mania?

He acknowledged for the first time that this was the want he'd worked the hardest for. Maybe he only had the gumption for one difficult goal. His job was decent, but not especially satisfying; his social life he once though of as vibrant and special, but he'd lately found that he was more dull than he thought he was; he was horribly lonely, and yet there was a potential partner ready and willing and only a few feet away. To improve anything required so much effort that it was easier to stifle. If he hadn't tried so hard to get hormones, would he be different? Had transitioning taught him the lesson that you *can* achieve a goal if you work very hard, but the achievement will still come with catches? This would explain why he was nonplussed by Nat's coming out; deep down, he knew it wouldn't do much. Then again, Nat *had* changed. Though his relations with Ty suffered, he was certainly more fun and pleasant than he'd ever been, and more attractive. He was louder, too, which was not necessarily a positive development but evident of a change in confidence. Nat was better at this than he was.

For the rest of the week, he felt fine. Not like his usual self, but someone more stable than who he'd been for the past several weeks. He stopped pinching his jaw line in the mirror on suspicion of "rounding out." He had more energy. He didn't get another period. He felt normal, and the unsure relief of getting the vial in his hands fizzled out into something like boredom. He was tired of this. Tired of himself.

17

2015

The morning after Madison's outburst, Lis pretended to be asleep long after she woke up, waiting to hear the noise of Madison leaving the dorm for library study. Under her covers, she pulled up her phone and saw the messages. *I heard something kind of fucked up last night, can you call me; hello; are you awake; hello; call me when you wake up.* Lis would have to face Tyler soon. She didn't want to make him wait long, especially when she suspected he only wanted to talk to her to cut ties, and if she was right that made her life a lot easier. But before she could speak to Tyler, she wanted to have a good day. She texted Ty, hoping he wasn't working. He was free, and had time to spend with her that afternoon, but she was willing to cut class to get there earlier. The walk to the train got her heart rate up and made her feel vigorous, so she walked further and got on at a station a few down from her usual stop, making herself sweat despite the cold. Soon, she would be able to make things with Ty official. She'd be his girlfriend. Not that today was the right day to do it, Madison's behavior had rattled Lis and made her worry about how this would affect their dorm situation next semester. On the train, Lis felt shaky, and her heart rate wouldn't slow even after she got a seat. Perhaps she hadn't realized how difficult an impending break-up could be. An understandable miscalculation, she thought, for someone ending their first relationship. He had been her first, and she was soon to spend a lot of energy regretting their time together. The tone of his texts from last night were more mournful than she expected them to be, and for the first time she began to feel guilty. That must have been why her stomach felt so hollow. She was eager to get to Ty's, and even more eager for Trevor to sober up and make her feel better about Tyler. If she could trust anyone to be blase about hurting a boy's feelings, it was Trevor.

Lis thought about a future in which she and Ty were mindlessly happy and she could thank Trevor for setting her free with his big mouth. She decided to not be at all mad for his indiscretion.

Once she arrived at Ty's apartment, he drew her in with a kiss. This felt so right. He offered her snacks and they sat on his couch to eat. No one else was home, and the peace of the living room was a great comfort. "Sorry it's so cold, the radiator doesn't come on until it gets dark," he said. Lis didn't mind; she pulled one of his couch blankets over her knees and let the rest of her sit up tall in the cool air. Though it was clear the windows hadn't been opened much due to the weather, it was not stale. The air was full of old cooking smells and candles, and with Max being a vegan that meant everything smelled like greens and soy wax. Lis's heartbeat finally began to calm down, and they got to talking as usual, about the friends they'd come to share and the places they went. Ty mentioned that Max had seen Trevor and Silvia two nights ago at a bar in Bushwick. "She said that Trevor was getting pretty messy, but I don't know. It seemed like Silvia was getting kind of worried about him," he said. Lis considered what to say here. She had an opening to come clean, though doing so with Ty before talking to Tyler felt wrong. Even so, she was nearly through. It was almost over. Maybe there was no reason to wait anymore. She wasn't scared, was she? "Oh, yeah I think I caught some of the aftermath."

"You saw him?"

"Sort of, he recuperated in my dorm and said a few things to my roommate that he probably shouldn't have said."

"Uh-oh. How bad?"

"Um. Not the worst. I mean, it's complicated."

"We don't have to talk about it."

"No, no it's fine. Uh, basically Trevor apparently mentioned you, and how we've been spending time together, and my room-mate had a whole conniption over it."

"Over me?"

"Well, she doesn't know who you are or anything but like, I was seeing this friend of hers that she's really obsessed with and it became like, I don't know like she was defending his honor or something."

"Oh gross. Was she like that when y'all broke up? I can't imagine wanting to live with someone like that when you're trying to cope with a relationship ending. None of her fucking business, you know." Ty misunderstood her; she could turn the conversation around, lie her way out and settle for a half-opened compromise in which she clued Ty in to Tyler's existence without having to admit anything further. And yet, the thought of lying to him any more than she already had made her heart feel like it was going to break.

"Um... I guess kind of. Things with this other guy, never officially ended like *that*, so I think I'm going to see how it plays out with her now."

Ty looked confused. "What do you mean?"

"This guy just, I think he might have been um,"

"Still dating you?"

"Kind of, but not, you know, I mean we hardly see each other anymore and I already knew we were going to break things off-"

"How long have you known you wanted to break up with this guy?" Ty's demeanor changed quickly. She noticed the turn of his shoulders in their sockets, curving downward and making him slouch more than usual. His torso curled at his stomach like a cave.

"Uh, since Halloween, I think."

Ty nodded like he got the answer he'd been waiting for. "Since we started fucking, you mean."

Lis didn't know how to answer. She only stared at him quietly. Ty looked around the apartment as if for an excuse. Finding none, he looked straight at her so intensely that she got scared. She could see he was left with no choice but to put her on the hook; she got the impression that he was deciding how obligated he was to have respect for himself. "You have to know that's fucked up," he said. Lis had to admit that she did, but she wanted to know what was getting her in trouble with him. "Which part?"

"Ah, fuck." He looked up at the ceiling and stayed quiet for a few moments. "This sucks." Pure disappointment melted down his face. Lis had never felt so ashamed. "I guess it was going to happen sometime," he said. "What?" She asked.

Ty looked at his thumbs, she could see his concentration and almost heard the sounds of his thoughts trying to decide what to say next. "Straight girls."

She was stunned that he could even think that. That he could have felt that way about all the time they'd spent together and the things she'd done with him. Then she questioned all she'd been doing for the past three months. It was all so big for her, but perhaps too small for him to notice. To be reminded of the distance between her self and her existence in the eyes of others —and her inability thus far to close that gap—made her feel flighty, like she wanted to run into the hall and zoom down Ty's street. Until now, she believed in something nigh on sacred be-tween her and Ty, but she now realized that she'd doomed them from the start. Could she blame him for only seeing the straight girl in her? No; what else had she given him? Lis couldn't bear to have him think that about her, that all she wanted out of him was the prestige of a good story. In truth she wanted much, much more. Her stomach sank when she got it into her head that Trevor and Silvia might also think of her as a tourist. Was being their friend enough to prove otherwise? If not, then what? What did she have to do?

She wouldn't be able to go out anymore. The realization made her heart break.

She stammered, spitting out all the apology words she had. "No, no please. That's not it. I don't even..." But Ty did not look at her. He didn't even look upset anymore. When he turned to her to ask her to leave, it was with a tired smile and an "I think you should head back."

On the way to the train, she slipped on the ice and nearly fell. The thrill of being knocked unsteady stopped her heart. She held it together for the train ride home and fell apart in her bed once she got back. She made a pile of herself, under the covers in her day clothes at four in the afternoon, and watched the sun set out her window through hot eyes. She didn't realize she was making noise until she heard someone else get home, walk up to the door, pause, and then quietly walk away. She thought it might be Madison, but changed her mind to Silvia, thinking that Madison wouldn't be able to resist seeing her cry. Lis's phone buzzed with another text from Tyler: *should I read into your silence?*

She did not want to call him or see him. She wasn't angry, she was weak. Too weak to put up with another chiding. She texted back, *i cant lie, im sorry.* Five minutes later, she read his next text: *fuck.* Ten minutes later, she read the next one: *maybe I shouldn't be surprised but this has never happened to me before.*

Of course it hasn't, she thought, because nothing bad ever happens to you. She read innocence in his messages; a sheer bewilderment that not only had Lis done this, but that he was hurting over it. Lis wondered if it was flattering herself to think that Tyler liked her the way she liked Ty. She knew it wasn't true, because Tyler would recover from this. He liked her and wanted her, but only if she wanted to be wanted back. He only fought the walls she put up in the most basic of ways, texting her to ask if she wanted to rehearse, or get coffee, but he never crowded her, never asked for answers. Maybe he just believed in ease. She wanted to be like that. She thought ease would be coming after today. She thought today was the backhanded solution to all her problems. Yet instead, she found that despite all hopes, she was the same person she had been when she woke up, no better.

2017

It was a fitful night of sleep Ty spent, listening to what sounded like a mouse running up and down the radiator pipes. Winter had already started, but the boiler was just now starting its winter schedule, and every night, while Ty tried to sleep, it clanged and whistled like it was going to blow. Normally it didn't bother him, but on that night in particular, he was jumpy.

He was thinking about Nat. Of all things one could want, a person was the most complicated. It was hard to remember why he had so many hangups about Nat. He could remember clearly when he stopped being infatuated with him, more clearly than he could remember what it was like when they first met. If he let himself go back there, it made him sad. Though most of his anger had faded into bitterness since 2015, he could remember old feelings of hope that cut him deep and sharp. When he first met Nat, he thought that he was going to have someone just for the sake of having them. It had been so easy to enjoy Nat's company, despite the things Nat didn't know. In fact, those holes of ignorance were charming. And it wasn't even that Nat was clueless; of course Nat was not quite what he seemed back then, as Ty would later find out, but even the little bits and pieces he gave away should have clued Ty in to what would come later. It wasn't anything Nat said that was significant, but the absence of curiosity. The first time they slept together, Nat didn't flinch.

He didn't ask anything, didn't seem surprised by Ty's body at all. It was so easy. Ty wanted so badly to think that he'd gotten lucky and found someone he liked who could just go with it, instead of having to have their hand held as Ty explained how he worked or why he looked the way he did. But then there was the boyfriend. And really, the boyfriend wasn't the problem. If Nat had just broken up with the guy behind Ty's back and carried on there probably wouldn't be an issue, but when Nat revealed the double life he'd been leading, it frightened Ty to realize that they now had a trust that meant Nat might tell Ty anything, even and especially the things he didn't want to hear.

He gave up on sleep, and instead rolled over and pulled his computer off the nightstand and into his lap. An investigative curiosity got hold of him, and if he wasn't sleeping anyway, he might as well sate his brain. He navigated to the iMessage app, found Nat's name, and scrolled. Since they now so rarely texted, it wasn't long before he found them, those big gray chunks of message from winter, 2015.

*I have been thinking a lot about you, and about the past few months, and about why ive been the way that i am, in general and with you. i know it hasnt been that long, but you *do* know me in a very different way than ive let anybody know me, which makes it seem like im someone completely different with you, but really im more me than i have ever been. I know you feel used, but I need you to understnad that that is *not* true. I have been trying for a really long time to ignore something about me that I havnt been ready to accept, and being with you let me feel like I was getting to it and you made me feel so good that I swear I never thought of being with you as lying or trying somethign on. To me, you were the first person I could be* *honest with, and I know that might sound like bullshit because technically I have not been *actually* honest with you but I hope that maybe you might get what I mean because maybe you went through this too. I mean, I *know* you went through this too, because im like you. Im trans too. And I think I have always known that but im trying to say it now, and I wanted you to be the first person I told. Not because you made me this way or anything but jsut because you were the first one I saw in real life. I knkw you had to have had someone like you when you did this, and maybe you know what that feels like, but I also *like* you. As a friend, as a crush, as someone im dating. That part is real, and I am real, and I know I havent told you the truth but in a way I also havent been lying to you because you might be the only person I dont lie to. I know you dont want to talk to me right now and I understand and I owe you an apology, so I just ask that you let me please.*

Ty had known. Ty had seen it coming, ever since that night he offered Nat a binder and saw the way it relieved him. Why even offer in the first place unless he'd identified something? The binder was a test. Knowing that someone is going to tell you something you don't want to know is a touchy burden; it makes you lash out in too-harsh ways that belie the cause of the real upset. Ty could have kept falling for Nat despite the boyfriend, but he was more worried that what was going to follow would be the admission that Nat only needed Ty for self-discovery, which had happened to queers better than him—he was too proud to let it happen to himself. He wanted things to stay easy. Being used was one thing, but what happened with Nat put Ty in the position of having to be supportive despite his disappointment, and that was worse. Eventually, looking at Nat began to feel like a pungent betrayal, like he was seeing something he really shouldn't.

However, Nat still wanted him, and that was something he couldn't handle either. How could Nat still want him? Ty remembered his first six months of coming out, the worst period of his life. He couldn't do that again, and to be with Nat would be like living with a puppy. A cruel thing to think, but he couldn't deny that there was something about Nat's newness that repulsed him. It could easily be mistaken for jealousy. Nat slid into transition so much easier than Ty. It took Ty years to feel okay letting his hair go past his ears, whereas Nat hadn't had a haircut in two years. On the night they hooked up, Ty watched him strip his binder right off—sometimes Ty still wanted to wear his. Maybe jealousy factored in a bit, but Ty was happy for Nat. That was the truth. He was so happy for Nat that in some ways, he wanted to be like him.

When Ty was in high school, he'd needed a release. This meant a haircut, which he got without his mother's knowledge. In minutes, his hair, which had always fallen below his shoulder blades, stopped touching his ears. The person who cut it was a friend of his, a girl with clippers, a kind heart, and a basement. She was from Staten Island, and the day of the haircut was the first day he'd been to her house. It felt right, to be on a separate land mass from home while she picked through his hair with a rattail comb, making sure she'd cut everything evenly. She didn't know what she was doing—that is, she gave a great haircut, but she thought the assignment was to remake Ty in the image of Pete Wentz for gay, not trans, reasons. For 2009, Ty looked great. In hindsight, the wide fang of hair over one eye was embarrassing, but looking at the old photos made him proud despite the cringe. It was the first thing he wanted that he didn't wait to get permission for.

His mother didn't speak to him when he got home, but the small group of friends he had at school loved it. There was one friend who seemed to especially like it, but Ty could never tell if it was flirtation or friendship. Most of the girls at his school had their best friends listed as their "wives" on Facebook, and the deepness of those friendships was often measured in physical intimacy. Could you hug your best friend? Kiss her? Had you seen her topless? Ty didn't have any friendships like that, because the lines were ill-defined. A good thick graphite can hold in a watercolor, but without it the paint runs over the page and you have to re-decide what you're making. If his best friend kissed his cheek, it wouldn't be cute. It would be scary, for both of them. Neither would be entirely sure who they were.

This time of year, the sun was supposed to be rising later and setting sooner, and yet at five am, there was a healthy stream of light pressing through the curtains. It reminded him of the sunrise through Nat's window, when he'd loped out of bed to go hide in his own room, a shameful memory. If he could do it over again, he hoped he might have the strength to stay in bed, maybe even hold Nat. Realistically, if he couldn't do that when he had the chance, what made him think he'd be able to do it now? He felt very weak, and ashamed, then maudlin. The kind of adult who spent this much energy on self-loathing was not the kind of adult he wanted to be. He wondered if he was the type of person who sucked all the energy out of the rooms he walked into. More than anything though, he wondered if the hole he'd dug himself into was too deep to be let out of. It was likely that even if he could find a well of inner strength from which to draw progress, he had fallen so far out of Nat's good graces that it was unlikely he'd be offered forgiveness.

That fear felt a lot like what was weighing on Ty now. When Ty realized what Nat was, the deep lines of hope that had been carved onto his heart dried up like desert ravines, and now they were scorched and ever-empty, waiting for a flood. To look at the problem head on was to stare down a dark corridor through himself. The ending of Lis and Ty was a story predicted by the hours in the bathroom, the bandages wrapped around his chest, the scars surgical and otherwise, the hatred he kept swallowed and didn't let out, the hatred he tried to release but couldn't for fear it would regain its losses. He could love himself as long as he forgot who he was; Nat was the opposite. Nat loved himself precisely because of who he was, and if it could be said that Nat loved Ty, it was for the same reason. Ty knew this, he knew it was behind every decision Nat had made back then. It was still true that Ty had been used, and though there was some good reason for him to feel betrayed, there were more and better reasons for him to feel adored. But to do so would be to reckon with himself, with Nat, with everyone else. He wasn't sure if he could, but he knew he couldn't go on the way he had been. He touched his face and felt the trail of the first tear he'd cried in two years. He and Nat were both boys who might not have been boys fifty years ago; who wouldn't care about each other the way they could now; two improbable creatures, the existences of which were less of a miracle and more of a why not.

18

2015

It was the night of the *Nutcracker*. Silvia was in a later act so Lis *could* go late, but she was afraid of the looks she'd get from the speech and movement coach who'd scolded her for arriving late to the previous semester's play when the 6 broke down and she had to walk four Manhattan blocks. She got ready in front of the full-length closet mirror, taking steps back and forth to adjust how close her view was, like adjusting the focus on a lens. She got on the train early, and got to school on time. The lights in the campus Starbucks were off, but clusters of students were seated in the lounge area in the dark, chatting and waiting to line up for the auditorium. These were drama students enjoying one of the few shows a year they didn't resent not getting a role in. It was one of the only shows they weren't allowed to audition for, as with all the ballets. To get an audition, you had to be a dance major; to be in the major, you had to have the years and years of training to pass the admission audition, while also having the stamina to have kept up good enough grades to enroll in a four-year liberal arts curriculum. The drama students, though expected to have a left foot and a right foot and the ability to twist them into jazz squares as needed, didn't have to be so ambitious; thus, this was the first show of the year they could truly enjoy. Lis was supposed to be that relaxed too, but while she was determined to put on a good show of support for Silvia, she was wound too tightly to sit with her classmates. The blow-ups of the past week left her with only two sympathetic ears, Silvia and Trevor, who might have only been kind to her because of their complicity in the schemes that had brought her so low. Lis loved Silvia and Trevor, but there was one friend she wanted more than anyone else, and she was terrified that she'd lost him. She needed to be alone, so she'd reserved a ticket for the night Trevor wasn't going, and she was glad that Silvia's responsibilities tonight and the demand for rest afterward meant that Lis was spared from making conversation. The thought of unclenching her jaw to breathe, let alone speak, was unbearable. The vice grip of her teeth was the only thing keeping gravity alive.

The tech crew had done a good job. They couldn't build a Rococo proscenium over the black box style auditorium, so instead they decorated every bit of stage not needed by the dancers with festive sculpture. The pieces were painted with candy colors; oversized children's toys made hills and monuments along the back of the stage, and a massive Christmas tree had been built and rigged to float down from the rafters with scene changes. It was lit with bulbs that Lis knew to be expensive and fragile,— one had to touch them with gloves on because the taint of human oil would shatter them on contact—how were they paying for all this? She looked at the twinkling silver plaques nailed to the back of all 400 seats in the auditorium, each bearing the name of a different donor.

Silvia was in several numbers as ensemble, but she was to have her big moment during the waltz of the flowers. Lis sat in her velour seat, getting warm. The house was supposed to be air conditioned year-round to counteract the stage lights; some people around her kept their scarves and sweaters on, but she'd already stripped down to her closest layer and thought she was in danger of breaking a sweat. It was her hair, or the boots. Something told her she wanted to look special that night, so she'd pulled out her most "Acting Major" black outfit and spread her favored purple on her lips. She looked like the girls the Arctic Monkeys sang about—good, because she was trying to. Her head started to hurt right when the first strokes of Silvia's suite began to play. It was a song she had heard so many times that she forgot this is where it came from. It was like a joke, that this masterpiece, rendered so flat by its being beaten to death by movie scores, came from *The Nutcracker*—to her, it was the equivalent of *Ride of the Valkyries* being composed for *The Grinch*. The big wide valleys of string instruments, the chirping flutes in response. Were they supposed to be real flowers or was this a metaphor for virgins?

Silvia's group popped out of the wings in lines, their feet hitting the floor like raindrops. Silvia never complained about her pointe shoes, but Lis wished she would. The dancers wore their major in their hair and under the bandages and bruises peeking out of their socks. Lis had seen Silvia's feet once or twice when she was late to class and had to change out of her dance shoes in the hall. They were gruesome, and it made her want to cry, that part of someone so lovely could be mangled so badly. How dare anyone put Silvia in such agony? Some ballerinas lost toenails. She thought of it like foot binding. She was so tired of hearing that beauty was pain.

Silvia stood out from the other dancers. Her arms held attention more tightly than any of the others, the way they made loops around her head and flew around in spirals while she jumped and landed, dropping all her weight onto her toes. Lis's head felt like it had its own nauseous stomach. The music was beautiful, and Lis loved to watch dancers. She liked to be enthusiastic about how great her school's shows were no matter whether or not they really were, no matter that she would never be in one. Silvia was marvelous. She was one soloist accompanied by two lines of dancers in long skirts and milkmaid braids. Silvia's costume looked nearly naked by comparison, just a pink leotard and slip in nearly the same tone as her skin. Lis looked for the sweating flush and the missing toenails, but they weren't there.

Silvia liked to tell a story about a ballerina whose skirt caught fire. She stood too close to a hot light and went up in flames. The only unburnt part of her were her face and breasts; her stays were burned into her back. Her mentor rubbed greasepaint in the burns, thinking it would soothe her until help arrived. For a year, she recovered in agony. At the end of that year, her wounds split back open and she died of septic shock.

The fire could have been prevented. There's a myth that there were no fireproof skirts at the time and that's what caused it, but it was the late 1800s, safe skirts were available. When asked, the ballerina spoke with her unburnt mouth to say that they did not move properly. The fireproof material sank right through the air —they were ugly. No theater yet demanded that ballerinas give up the flammable skirts, and the burnt ballerina maintained that she had the right to burst into flames if she wanted to. No one disputed her for decades. Silvia's skirt tonight was not fireproof, it was the stage lights that stopped being made with gas.

Silvia's toes pierced the floor of the stage like a tattoo needle to the rhythm of the tweeting music, interspersed by long leaps. She spun on one foot like a drill, locking her eyes on a spot in front of her, swiveling her head around before the turn broke her neck. She looked so beautiful. Lis knew, watching Silvia, that the reason she would never be put in one of her school's plays was because when she was on stage, she did not make performance look easy. Lis was not moved by classical music until that night. She could see the tips of bows in the barely-concealed orchestra pit thrumming up and down, shoulders of the suit-clad baby-faced musicians swaying back and forth like they still enjoyed making this thing they lost so much to. Lis did not know any of them because they only knew each other, and only from the hours spent in the practice room. The back of her throat began to hurt. It was tightening, getting ready to start sobbing. She clenched her jaw to stop it, but then her head hurt more.

Crying came against her will. It was so hot, the tears felt awful, like grease instead of water. The tears would mix into her makeup and dry into a gritty crust. She hoped she still looked alright, but in her mind's eye she saw her splotchy red skin and wet face seated in between two well-dressed adults—parents or donors—and became preemptively embarrassed. She wanted so badly to get out. She was thinking of how nice the cold air would feel on her face, and how she could wait until she got outside to put her coat on so her sweating skin could dry up and calm down before she went home. Would Silvia see her walk out? No, no. She would be too absorbed. Maybe Lis could just wait until she was in the wings. She tried to hold it together until she reached her limit, and when she did, she redefined the limit.

She managed to stay seated until the number ended, and when everyone applauded, she made like she was going to the bathroom. Silvia's phone, tucked in her purse in the dressing room, buzzed with a text: *you were amazing! had to leave early, i got my period. love you!* Unsatisfied with that, Lis sent another: *you were beautiful. so fucking beautiful.*

The halls were empty as she left. The guards at the security desk couldn't see her face as she speed-walked through the doors. The street was cold and clear. The winter air was slightly damp from a light snow that was falling in limp wet flakes. The wind blew and became stiff little spears, concentrating and piercing Lis in the chest, where her scarf didn't protect her. It was the most soothed she'd ever been. When she got back to the dorms, she turned red from the warmth rushing to her, clinging to her. She stood in front of the mirror for the second time that night in her coat, waiting for a long time before she began to undress. She looked at her face, now weathered from the cold and the makeup that had steeped in her tears and sweat and then cracked in the wind on the way home. She admired herself in the outfit she picked out so carefully, and she considered herself, imagining the things that could be said about her in the next ten years.

Lis is so pretty. Lis has a boyfriend. Lis has had lots of boyfriends. Lis is good at makeup. Lis is very talented. Lis is going to be in movies.

Lis is an ingenue. Lis has lots of money. Lis has two beautiful children. Lis really knows how to maintain a work-life balance. Lis proves women really can have it all. Does anybody else think Lis looks kind of like Veronica Lake? Lis can paint her nails without getting paint on the cuticle. Lis does not blow dry her hair. Lis believes in a woman's right to choose. Lis is doing great. Lis has nothing left to learn. Lis is all done.

2017

In Ty's home neighborhood, there were a lot of houses converted into multi-family homes. Since the conversion, housing law required them to have fire escapes, and the cheapest thing to do was jerry-rig some iron baskets over the siding. Given the irregular shape of the houses, the ladders of the escapes bit into roofs and windowsills. The gutter of one house had a big chunk ripped out of it to make room for egress, so when it rained, the water poured over the iron from two directions. The structure was now so rusted that it looked like it could be chewed off. The fire escape off of Ty's bedroom was slightly more stable, enough so that he felt comfortable putting his body weight on it, even when the rain made the iron slats treacherous. Now that he knew Nat could see him so clearly from his bedroom window, he found himself posing with a cigarette he'd snuck from Lita's pack. He wondered if Nat was watching and if he noticed Ty being artificial. It was presumptuous, he knew, to think Nat had even formed a habit of observing him that frequently.

Anyway, it was cold. October was right around the corner, instilling Ty with some boldness. Summer made him feel suffocated, whereas the turn of the season operated on him like the reverse of hibernation. As his cigarette dwindled, Ty felt like knocking on Nat's door. He gave a parting glance to the dying weeds in the alley concrete's canyon, and made for Nat's door. Nat didn't keep it locked, and invited Ty in right away. Sure enough, he was sitting at his desk, facing the window. Maybe he'd watched Ty finish his cigarette and turn back inside, maybe he knew to expect him. From the door, Ty asked, "How have you been?" Nat's eyes were not tired, but sleepy, like he was waking up. "Fine. I don't know, I think I expected to be more emotional." His voice was soft and crinkling, like a piece of tissue paper.

Ty nodded, "I get that. I saw all those videos of people crying when they woke up, but it just didn't affect me like that." Nat looked at him, then at the sunset, then back at him, like he was deciding something, and then he said, "I used to cry so much when I was little. Like every day, until I was thirteen or something, but then I just stopped."

Ty hadn't expected a confession, but Nat was more forthcoming than Ty gave him credit for."Yeah?"

"The last time I cried was two years ago, and the last time before that was probably eight years ago."

Ty had once looked up why humans cry. It's a self-soothing behavior, one that releases endorphins and oxytocin to ease us through the pain. Two years since Nat's last cry, and a six-year drought before that. Nat either had a constitution or a clog. The fact that the last time Nat was brought to tears had been two years prior was not lost on him. He considered how Nat must have felt, on the brink of something huge and suddenly shunned by the closest living example of what he wanted to be. Ty had come into this room with a foggy idea of getting to the bottom of something, and Nat's sudden tenderness emboldened him enough to plainly ask, "Why did we have sex, Nat?"

Nat shrugged his shoulders and rolled his eyes, but not derisively. In his gesture was the knowledge that though he didn't have any hangups himself, Ty's need to understand his own actions made sense. "Because we wanted to," he said in a confident voice. "I didn't think about it that much, honestly. I don't think you did either, because I know you, and I know that if you had a taken a second to talk yourself out of it you would have." Ty knew this was true. If he'd paused for even a moment, he would've stopped. That night, he'd done exactly what he wanted to, and only because he'd sidestepped his hedge maze of a mind. But still, he wasn't entirely satisfied by that answer, because though for him it was a matter of getting out of his head, he thought maybe Nat had been more deliberate. After all, he felt like he'd been seduced. "You really didn't think about it?" He asked. Nat looked straight into Ty's eyes. "No, I didn't. Believe it or not, I just thought we were having a good time and the moment was right," he said, and he it was clear that he meant it.

"What do you mean?"

"Ty, you know that I regret what happened back then. And like, I get it. I put myself in your shoes and I can guess what you were feeling but, I've always wondered. If you knew why I used to live the way I did—I mean, you *do* know why I used to live the way I did. I guess I've always been confused as to why, after I got back here, after I started coming to the bars again, why it was still a problem. Not that I think I'm so special, but I think we like each other, and I figured that once you realized what I really was that it would make things better, not worse."

"How have they been worse?"

"I know we're friends, but I can tell that I annoy you. And I know that I'm annoying, but I'm not *that* annoying. Clearly there's something you've continued to tolerate about me. I mean, I live here."

Ty got quiet, or rather, quieter than he already was. His mind was racing back and forth across a gym floor. He thought about what he'd discussed with Silvia, about growing up, something he wanted to do very much. He thought about Lita, the things she picked on him for that he'd never noticed about himself. He never thought he was uptight until he met Nat, and he wondered if his friends from high school could see him now, would they think he hadn't changed? He didn't want to be like that, he didn't want to be closed off, or in denial. Without realizing it,—or not wanting to believe it— he'd entered a new phase of wanting. Experience could teach him that the only thing to do for this is accept the want and ask for it be satisfied, but it was a lesson that didn't stick. He was disappointed with himself, since this was a relatively petty want compared to what he'd already gotten for himself. He was disappointed that his compulsion toward self-denial and punishment had warped his brain and his connections to others again. Nat was right; he was annoying, but not *that* annoying, and his annoyances were nothing Ty couldn't recognize from his own past, things that Nat would grow out of as long as he stayed with the crowd he was in. Again, time was wasted that could have been spent happily.

"I owe you an apology," he said.

Nat looked surprised. "What for?"

"I've been an asshole to you."

Nat waved his hand, "Come on, you're not that bad."

"No, I am. I'm harder than I need to be on you, I put you down, I give you weird mixed signals…"

"Ty—"

"I'm sorry. I do like you, and I *am* your friend."

Nat waited a few seconds as if he expected Ty to say more. He brought up his hand in the "go-on" gesture. "And?"

Ty felt sweat emerge on his chest. "And what?"

Nat half-laughed. "Do we have the time for *both* of us to be bad at this?"

They exchanged a serious look, and Ty tried to let go of the last shred of lockdown, the last part of himself that didn't think it could give Nat what he wanted, to acknowledge that what he and Nat wanted was the same. He looked at the buttons of Nat's shirt. "Can I see?" Nat nodded, "sure," and began to unbutton himself. He let the shirt fall around his shoulders like a dressing gown. He didn't have the scars Ty did. Nat's surgeon instead removed the tissue via incisions made around his nipples, so the only visible marks were two tiny cross-shaped exit wounds on each side of his ribcage from the drains. Ty put his hand up to touch, and waited for a glance from Nat to tell him it was okay. He touched his fingertips to the center of Nat's chest, Nat shivered. When Ty's hand twitch away, Nat said, "It's ok, it just feels weird still, but they said pressure would help the nerves reconnect."

Ty relaxed, and nodded. "I remember."

Ty opened his hand to press it flat against Nat's chest, and watched his breath ruffle the hair there. Nat breathed against Ty's hand. "Can I ask you something?"

"Sure," Ty said.

"What do you imagine when you think of getting what you want?"

Ty looked at Nat, at his own hand with Nat's hairs between his fingers, the post-its in the bookmarks on Nat's desk, the view from his window. He did not think before answering.

"This."

Acknowledgements

IN ORDER OF APPEARANCE

- My mom, for bringing me here and keeping me here.
- My dad, for helping my mom get me here.
- My brother, for being my teammate and an endless source of entertainment.
- Victor, my other brother, for keeping me alive.
- My younger sister, for motivating me to be someone she can be proud of.
- AJ, for being the guy to show me what love could be and how it can transform into friendship.
- Miss Malice, my first reader, my mentor, my surrogate big sister, and ultimate femme dyke icon.
- Miwa, for being a tireless example of strength, generosity, vibrance, and skrink.
- Ponii, for shocking me out of my shell and driving me to be a better freak.
- Violet, my first feline child, who taught me how to love little creatures.
- My youngest sister, who is only one, but adorable.
- Nico, the love of my life, and the designer of this book's beautiful cover.

- Moi, my favorite gay dog stepson.
- Pippin, who didn't really do anything, but is very cute.

Thank you too, to all those who donated to help me complete this project and publish this book.

Alex Nolos is a writer and editor born, raised, residing, and intending to die in Brooklyn, NY. He performs as the drag king Orson Price on a sporadic basis. His other work can be read in *Catapult*, *Hominum Journal*, and *Wrongdoing Magazine*. He would like you all to tip your kings, queens, and bartenders.